Michael Giacometti has been a computer programmer, a trekking guide, an arts worker, a bus driver. In 2008 he pulled a cart weighing twice his own body weight across the Simpson Desert, becoming the first (and only) person to complete an east–west crossing, solo and unassisted. His writing has appeared in *Meanjin*, *Island*, *Cordite*, *Wild*, and anthologies including *Cracking the Spine: Ten short Australian stories and how they were written* (Spineless Wonders, 2014). He won the NT Literary Award for Poetry 2012 and 2017, and in 2016 he was the Regional Emerging Writer-in-Residence at the Newcastle Writers Festival. *My Life & Other Fictions* is his debut publication. He lives in Alice Springs with his partner and camp dog.

Spineless Wonders
PO Box 220 STRAWBERRY HILLS
New South Wales, Australia, 2012
www.shortaustralianstories.com.au

First published by Spineless Wonders 2017

Text © Michael Giacometti 2017
Cover design and typesetting by Bettina Kaiser.
Edited by Josh Mei-Ling Dubrau.
Publishing interns, Kate Potter and Bec Cameron.
Publisher, Bronwyn Mehan.

Typeset in Adobe Garamond Pro
Printed and bound by Lightning Source Australia

National Library of Australia Cataloguing-in-Publication entry
My Life & Other Fictions /Michael Giacometti
1st ed.
978-1-925052-32-9 (pbk)
A823.4

Australian Government

This project has been assisted by the Australian Government through the Australia Council,
its arts funding and advisory body.

Through these deliberately unconnected impressions I am the indifferent narrator of my autobiography without events, of my history without a life. These are my Confessions and if I say nothing in them it's because I have nothing to say.

What could anyone confess that would be worth anything or serve any useful purpose? What has happened to us has either happened to everyone or to us alone; if the former it has no novelty value and if the latter it will be incomprehensible…. What I confess is of no importance because nothing is of importance.

FERNANDO PESSOA, THE BOOK OF DISQUIET 25

MY LIFE
& Other Fictions

MICHAEL GIACOMETTI

For K (1938–1978)

Contents

my abbr.d life

My ma is a self-mutilating alcoholic.

She was beautiful, granny says with a hint of a smile shaking her head, but wilful. I see it. Her slender emu legs, her sexy doggy-dance, her don't-mess-with-me glare. Might be all you see is lazy bloodshot eyes, tits falling out of a dress four sizes too large, soiled bandages on her forearm and head. Might be the stink of grog and sweat and meat and piss of her that sticks to everything that has you puking up air. Piss off, you growl like she is some mongrel camp dog. But when I smell those rich scents, thick and juicy as a steak from off a killer, I can't help but giggle and thrash about because I know I'm gonna see my ma.

But I don't see her much. Granny grows me up. Like in old times, she says, the old ones stay in camp and teach the young ones while the women go out and gather food for them all. Only difference is ma gathers nothing for us, no matter how much granny and aunty boss her like willy-wagtails at a crow. She gamble all her sitdown money at cards trying for the big kitty. Maybe she win enough for a fridge or a meat tray. When the money gone she joins in singing the green can dreaming that wanders from tree to tree along the sandy riverbed.

1

Granny says ma wants to drown her sorrow because her ma was stolen from her, but ma isn't sinking, all that grog it keep her afloat. Even when uncle lie on her she don't go under. Thinking he is a stone she clings to him, but must be he is full of air and she floats. Even his fists are puffy clouds. Her skin soak up all they rain down on her.

Ma is swimming in that river of grog when I jump into her belly. My milk is 90 proof. I emerge from her cave like a joey: undersized, soft and squishy right through. No words form on my tongue. I crawl about when other kids same age as me are kicking the footy and taking hangers.

Uncle take me many times. I am promised to him at birth. But he take me, he take me from aunty's breast. He smell of booze and ganja and mulga smoke. The uncles play a dvd showing naked people doing grunting things. Cousins sit on the floor in front of the tv like the best kids in class. Uncle laughs. He call me marsupial mole. He say, I speared me little mole. The uncles laugh too. Their spears are hard and sharp. They move with purpose.

When ma is sober she sometimes bring hot chips with gravy and a cool drink from the community shop. My gum bleeds. When ma leaves I cling to her. She growl at me and punch her love into bruises that flower darker than my skin. I try to make them last until ma touch me again.

I don't resist when my cousin-sister cut a cola can in half, pierce a couple of holes in the jagged rim and put a piece of wire through. She hang it over my head like a feed bag and pour in a little bit purple liquid from a plastic bottle. Don't drink it, she signs with a hand and nose, sniff. Like that mob over there, she points—the skinny, shuffling, mumbling ghost kids with bulging eyes.

It is sweet. I sit beneath mulga near a deep hole. Ma is beside me. She puts a coolamon on my lap, heavy with honey ants. I slurp on the sweet golden drops and smile and snuggle into the drowsy warmth of ma.

The notice in the paper call me 'no name' out of cultural respect, or shame. Iloveyousoverymuchmychild, ma slurs and cuts her bare breast deep and bleeds into dust. Aunties plastered with white clay drone wetly and tear fistfuls of tangled hair from their head. They do it for me.

My name is Shantitia Hames.

I was six years old.

At Failure Creek

From the extraordinary and deceptive appearances caused by mirage and refraction, it was impossible to tell what to make of sensible objects, or what to believe on the evidence of vision ... The whole scene partook more of enchantment than reality ... all was uncertainty and conjecture in that region of magic.
Edward John Eyre, *Journals of Expeditions of Discovery into Central Australia*

Within the sanctity of my canvas tent, away from the prying eyes of the men, I lie on a stretcher like a corpse in an open coffin. From outside, the ragged murmuring of the men ... *I shall not want* ... penetrates the porous fabric. Occasional coughs and silences punctuate the nightly prayer. The men's recitation only gains unity as they ... *walk through the valley of the shadow of death* ... but it is fear, not fervour, that gives them strident voice, the ever-present fear of being buried in a forgotten grave one thousand miles from home amid the illegible features of this barren land.

Again the shell calls for me, just as the men hum and spit out the final line. I take it from the velvet-lined box that I keep always on my person and hold it to my ear. From its open mouth I hear my name on the breeze, the haunting waves of the yet-to-be-discovered inland sea. It calls to me and only me, calling me to cast off from the red sand of that alien beach.

In my clumsy fingers and the honeyed light of a solitary candle, the shell glows. So often have I examined its surface for clues of its origin that I can re-create the shell entirely with closed eyes: the slight flavour of clay; the white kaolin-like coating; the concentric circles drawing the eye in to a central point; the file-like grooves—growth lines like girth circles of trees, cold to touch. It is my amulet on this venture that my lineage and my rank and my faith have anointed for me.

The tent flap rustles in the still night, as if speaking: 'Captain, sir. You sent for me?' My fingers curl around the shell, guarding it from sight.

Since the unfortunate death of my deputy several months ago, Mr Browne has been a more than capable and dependable adjutant. In my weakened and near-blind state, I cannot thank him too much, for as God is my witness, I know he too suffers from the deficiency that afflicts sailors and land explorers alike. It pains him greatly to sit in the saddle, his sore and bloody gums make it difficult to chew, and he is obliged to eat flour and water boiled; and though they are concealed always by his trousers, I know his thighs, like mine, are covered in dark purple spots. Browne neither complains about his afflictions nor shirks his responsibilities. He performs his duties admirably, enduring the privations of exploring without expectation of praise or reward.

By my reckoning it is Sunday, and since it pains me to hold a pen for any length of time beyond necessary note-taking, he has come for me to dictate my weekly letter to my dear wife in Adelaide. I pray that soon I will be able to despatch a man with these letters, and a copy of my official journal and chart proclaiming my success in reaching the Centre.

Before commencing to write, Mr Browne wads up a ball of bush snuff, a kind of chewing tobacco that we have observed the natives to hold in their mouth or behind their ear. They call it 'pechery' and it is made from the leaves of a plant whose identity they would not disclose mixed with the ash from the bark of a eucalypt. It delivers a hot chilli sensation to the tip of the tongue reminding me of my childhood in India. He hands it to me and I work it into my gum with saliva, spitting occasionally, as an Indian would with betel. The narcotic effect quickly relieves my aches and frees my tongue.

O my Dearest Charlotte, I am aged beyond my fifty years from this infernal land. I feel that I have done you and our cherished daughter a great disservice in undertaking this enterprise. For though I have penetrated this continent further than any before me, in these thirteen months I am yet to discover anything of use to civilised man.

This execrable land is the very antithesis of the New Jerusalem I seek to discover. The fearsome interior is akin to the forge of Hell, a place where even the Lord's esteemed servant Job would be hard pressed to continue supplication.

In earlier reports I detailed the ordeals I have thus far endured, but Dearest, please indulge me as I recount them again here, for those horrors now seem like a longed-for bliss: for there I was entombed in a communal pit for month upon month of thermometer-bursting temperatures, the only water for hundreds of miles in any direction greedily consumed by man and beast and sky until the skiff threatened to ground. I led prayers daily. I prayed underground for springs to spout geysers. I prayed in the boat for rivers to run. I prayed in the mottled shade of the tall gums for limbs and debris to wedge at the height of two men above. I prayed on the rocky hill for a pinnacle to reach the heavens. Dark clouds formed and the flies amassed in humid expectation, filling our eyes, our noses and mouths. The waving of hands and hats swept not the flies but the clouds away.

Five months of God-less silence passed. Like King David, I was deserted by He who once held me in favour.

Yet I prayed. I prayed.

The providential rain came at dawn, exploding like a cannonade. The skiff buckled with the first salvo, and as our pit became a well, the boat was swept downstream by the deluge and shattered on the rocks of an ephemeral rapid. I managed to salvage a fragment of oar and a length of canvas sail-cloth with which to furnish a new craft.

I pause. The shell feels like a block of ice in its fisted prison and the whitewash of waves now roars in my ears as if driven by an approaching storm. I raise a hand to squeeze like a pincer at my temples, to silence the white noise, to ensnare those images and memories that I must not give voice.

Eyre, my very good friend, who rightly dedicated his exploratory journals to me, gave me additional proof of the existence of the inland sea. Having ventured further inland than any before him (albeit, to a point that I have now far outdistanced), Eyre described a gentle sloping of the land from the south and east towards the centre of the continent—in a direction opposite to the course of the magnificent rivers I discovered in my earlier expeditions—and within this catchment there exists the watercourses of several great rivers, hundreds of yards across, all dry. These facts gave me heart, for I have the highest regard for Eyre—in his untiring perseverance and dedication to geographic observation he ranks second to none but me. But they rated as secondary in my estimations, for he said he had even further proof.

He took my elbow and led me to a corner of his anteroom where no-one would be able to overhear. His eyes were wide and white as he lifted his face to mine. Two words flew from his whispering lips into my soul.

'Gulls, terns.'

He drew back to register the import of the words that had already seized me. Gulls and terns! Seabirds! In the centre of the continent! By trained force my face remained impassive.

Eyre went on to describe large flocks of gulls and terns flying low overhead in a nor nor westerly direction towards the unknown centre, so many that the air was thick with their raucous calls and the smell of salt, the ground coated in their guano. 'There is the proof for you,' Eyre concluded in a whisper, knowing that my age and my retirement from exploring were no barrier to desire.

But Eyre's report of the shrill, salty cries of seabirds was not all that I received that night. With the fire of discovery burning within, I was, quite inexplicably, entertained by desires of the flesh. As I rode home that evening I paid a visit to a lubra in the native's shanty beside the river. From the geography of her person, the lubra revealed a luminous object the size of her thumbnail—a pale shell that shone brilliantly in the moonlight. In pidgin she spoke of its provenance while I turned the weightless object about. 'From the big water, northways, longaways, in that sand country.' She flung her hand repeatedly in the correct direction, not looking at me. I licked the salt from the shell's entrance, held the opening to my ear. Later, as I rode home, the gentle wash of waves propelled me on.

I feel the waves splash gently on my face like a cleansing morning wash, and pray that I have not exposed myself and spoken aloud these personal private thoughts. With a clearing harrumph, I hear my voice continue.

Dearest, man needs water to survive, yet as that single oasis became my goal, this dry creek where tonight I am encamped—which I have named for my good friend Eyre—propels me onward against the current.[1]

Without green feed the horses are now reduced to walking skeletons. It pains me to climb into the saddle where I slump forward as if bearing a great weight on my shoulders. I can barely lift my head and so must navigate a path through the spinifex by studying the patterns in the sand beneath my suspended feet, a method as effective as divining tea leaves in a china cup. My feet blister in the hot stirrups, my nose runs bloody, and my parched throat constricts with the bitter metallic-green bile of copper.

It is but September yet the furnace of summer hastens. Today, a great flock of green budgerigars flew over heading south. I wondered

---

1. Government cartographers chose not to accept the name Eyre, instead giving it the epithet by which it is now generally known. [Ed.]

for how long they had been flying and whence their migration to better-watered lands began. If there is not water enough for the flocks of birds, then how will there be enough for thirsty men and horses who require gallons? Every day that I delay turning back I risk not reaching the failing waters before they are reduced to stinking mud that even pigs would refuse and my safe passage back to the Depôt on Preservation Creek, that prison oasis in the blue mulga, is cut off.

Despite the emasculated clouds overhead today, I was able to take celestial observations for the first time in over a week. By my reckoning, I am 350 miles north of Eyre's Mount Hopeless, scarcely a degree from the Tropic and within 150 miles of the Centre of the Continent. The proximity to my objective is the whip and spur.

Yet again, I have exhausted all reasonable and logical avenues of advance. The most hazardous course, that which offers no promise of return, must again be the route outlined for me by Divine Providence. I will do all that human perseverance and diligence can achieve to accomplish my duty.

I am resolved to chart a course west directly over the fiery red sand ridges, those fabulous land waves that tower in unbroken formation above this dry valley camp. West …

The sound of paper scratching halts. Without looking I feel Browne's gaze directed at me like an exclamation. I keep speaking. It is his duty to follow.

… west it must be: to the Centre and the inland sea; to glory.

'Leave it there, Mr Browne. I may add some lines in my own hand afterward,' I say, dismissing him with a wave. 'And Mr Browne,' I add, catching him at the threshold, 'inform the men of my intentions for the morrow.'

The tent flap closes and his slow footfalls are carried away. As I rub my eyes, I recapture the dream of last night. The images play out on the theatre stage of my closed eyes: the streets of Adelaide crowded with women and men, cheering and waving their hats in the air; a brass band playing on the steps of Parliament; a column of conquering explorers atop strutting beasts advancing triumphantly up the broad avenue; and there, at the procession's head, I hold aloft the Union Jack, neatly hand-stitched in silk by the Adelaide Ladies, tied with double bowlines to the oar six feet above my blue-crowned head.

The sound of swearing and pots crashing startles my mount. The band conductor turns his head in consternation. The crowd steps back as I rein in my horse. The music degenerates into a storm of swelling waves that break over the crowd—slack-jawed and staring—as the procession is transformed. The explorer heroes have vanished. In their stead, some motley specimens stagger along Rundle Street to the slow clatter of un-shod feet. At their head, slung between two horses, all ribs and mange, a makeshift stretcher bears a living skeleton, prone, unable to rise. In the hard sunlight his skin is the grey-pink of salted meat. His flesh peels and curls. Salt crystals gleam on his lips. His cratered eyes, open and unmoving, are red as bushfire sunset. Gripped in his talon-like fingers is a jewellery box, open and empty.

I recoil from the damned vision. My eyes, my hands, jerk open. The treasured shell roars and rolls free. 'No, no, no,' I chant. I clutch at the falling fragile thing like a man overboard grasping at an oar held out for his rescue. 'No,' I say as I reveal the catch. 'No,' I sob to the silence.

I bring my hand in close to examine the remains. I follow the spiralling path from the shell's entrance, leading further and deeper into the labyrinth, gradually closing in on all sides, further and deeper and further still, until there is nowhere to go, nowhere, a dead end, and a retreat by the same spiralling path is the only option. The fragments fall to my chest, then finally to earth as I roll groaning onto my side.

I grab the fine goose quill, dip it in the open well and commence to write, but my hand cramps. The pen falls onto the paper; my wasted hand snatches at the feathered stem and the roaring inside my head finally escapes the lock of my lips.

Mr Browne is suddenly here, his arm outstretched towards me, fingers trembling; the men's ghastly faces are framed around his head in the open canvas flap. With difficulty I look down.

The letter. The remains of the shell beside it.

Dark ink snakes across the page, leaving a river turned to salt by my spittle and tears, and a large blot, shaped like a question or a decision. Already dry.

undersize

inspired by Luke Shelley's hexaptych 'Dad's Mullet'

Let the fossil record show: one *Mugil cephalus* (known variously as hardgut mullet, sea and river mullet, or black, grey, striped, and jumping mullet) trapped within the opaque layers of fine white sand and silt laid down by a tidal estuary during the Ogilocene. The siltstone sheet is cracked into six tiles or plates, each being almost square in shape, with starched edges and roughed-off corners.

There is much that remains unknown about the mullet. What was its life like? How did it die? How many mullet escaped the estuarine time capsule? Regarding such matters the fossil record is incomplete.

But I was there. And the mythology of the mullet lingers in my family like the stench of gutted fish. No amount of scrubbing can get rid of it. So, to set the record straight, I'll tell you the story of this fish, the story of the mullet.

Those plates were the best that we could afford, and even though they were second-hand from the op shop, they were an extravagance. Many a Sunday meal was served on them, but the one that

I will never forget was on the day that Dad first took me on the early morning mullet run.

In the pre-dawn darkness Dad loaded the tinnie: thermos, bait-bucket, fishing rods, empty bucket, net, spotlight. Within minutes we were away from the jetty, motoring upstream towards the mouth of the tidal estuary, where salt water meets fresh and the tidal currents stir up the algae and sediment that the mullet prefer.

'A vegetarian fish,' Dad shouted over the wind and engine whine. 'Gizzard like a chicken so it can grind and digest plant food.' I could already taste the lean and firm fishy meat. The way Mum grilled it in butter with a squeeze of lemon would have us four kids hanging round the kitchen salivating, and the neighbour's cat mewing and scratching at the door for scraps.

As we met the incoming tide we slowed, looking and listening for the telltale signs of mullet. The silver scaly flash. The heavy leaping splash. The mullet were running and I'd soon be eating their briny flesh.

We cast. We caught. The bait bucket emptied. The empty bucket filled with flapping then stillness. We motored back in, smiles sharper than gutting knives. At least, that's how some others tell the story.

I landed a 4-pounder on my first cast. Dad was impressed, though not to be outdone. He hooked an undersize one, threw it back. Then another. And another. And another.

For an hour he baited and caught, I netted, he measured and threw back. For that long hour my hunger and his desperation grew until both threatened to overload the tinnie and tip us into the dark water.

We headed in.

On the way home Dad stopped at the local take-away. 'Stay in the car,' he growled. I stared out the side window. The wind was chopping the bay, stirring up the sand. Dad returned. He tossed the hot parcel at me. 'See if you can hold on to that,' he said, then not another word. Not one. All the way home.

I caught the look on Mum's face when we came through the door.

'Don't ask,' Dad said, glancing sharply at me.

It was a quick clean cut from my throat the full length of my belly. Dad slumped into his chair. He could see that mullet draped across our six plates, filling them entirely, his knife and fork and teeth working away at it.

And I could still see that mullet too.

My first kill. On the way back in to the jetty I lifted it out of the bucket. Standing at the prow, I held that dead mullet before me like it was an offering to the gods.

There came a hoarse cry like a strangled gull. A sudden sideways jolt. And then the surprising slap of water. The mullet drifted free. I watched it sink as I too sank beneath the dark water. Dad dived in. Down he swam. Down past me. Down after that dead mullet as it settled deep in the sandy bottom and the silt covered it like a shroud.

Dad surfaced, gasping. All he caught in his net was me.

Geometry

Practice doesn't make perfect—only perfect practice makes perfect.
Ron Barassi

The oval lights are on and the team jogs a couple of slow laps together. On the near wing the coach casts four unequal shadows and calls *Bring it in* and the players wheel and run to the coach. They huddle close, shoulder to shoulder, crowding around the coach like a convent of king penguins. The last to arrive drops to the ground and does ten rapid push-ups.

The thirty-plus players divide into three roughly equal groups: one in the goal square, the other two on each forward flank just beyond the 50-metre line. The three groups thus form an equilateral triangle whose vertices (A, B and C) are about 60 metres apart. Plastic cones, like those used by road crews, mark the points so the triangle is not distorted by spread or creep.

From the goal square (A) a ball is kicked out to a player on the lead from one flank (B1) while another player from the same cone (B2) backs him up. The player marks and the one backing up sprints by and calls for the handball, which he receives. He kicks to the calling and leading forward on the other flank (C1). The forward marks, or does not, and the player backing up the forward (C2) calls for and takes the handpass, or picks up the crumbs. He runs his full measure and snaps at goal. Those that kick the ball keep running on until they get to the next cone—A to B, B to C, and C to A—then regather their breath with the other players waiting their turn. The next ball is kicked into play from the goal square (A) at the same time that the forward C1 attempts to mark.

It remains to be proved that the kicking, marking and running skills of A, B1, B2, and C1 equal, or in any way influence, the accuracy of kicking for goal by C2.

Prior to the final *run it in* and jogging a couple of cool-down laps, the last exercise of training is circle work. It runs for the term of a game's quarter plus time-on.

Players spread radially around the ground in clusters of twos and threes, forming a rough circle around the centre square, a circle whose axes run from wing to wing and from the hole between full-back and centre half-back to the corresponding hole at the other end of the ground between centre half-forward and full-forward. The drill begins with one football. Once the wheel starts rotating, a second ball is added, and sometimes a third.

From the wing the ball is kicked long. *Mine* shouts one player about fifty metres away on the flank. He leaps alone and the backward-spiralling ball lands precisely in the mirrored hands of his extended arms. As he lands on his feet and brings the ball down to chest level, two players, already sprinting and shouting, run past him, one closer to the centre, the other on the boundary side. *Hands-hands-hands* they both call. He handballs with the left or right to one of them. That player gives with the hands to the other runner and he takes a few fast paces before he spots a player across on the outer flank leading and calling for the ball, and then kicks cleanly and keeps running on to back up any fumble. The ball is marked and handballed to a smaller running player who kicks to the outer wing. And so on. Around the forward flank to the wing and around the back flank to the outer wing, players calling and kicking and shouting and running and handballing and supporting, one ball passing through and then, with hands on hips, turning to set for the next ball approaching, continuing like a perpetual motion machine for twenty minutes without even once trying to add to the scoreboard.

The two drills are practised without alteration or amendment every training session, three times a week. Their repetition is designed to create unconscious habits. Run. Back up. Keep the ball moving by hand or foot.

Come Saturday afternoon, after the final siren of another season, past players and die-hard supporters dissect what could have been, over another beer.

Position by position, we are better. Our finesse, our fitness, our teamwork are all superior. But...

But no-one knew. Not the coaching staff, not the players or their wives and girlfriends. Not the supporters. And certainly not the media.

The boys will be better for this, the coach said after the loss. *Next year*, many of the boys said to each other.

Yes, next year: same aspiration, running the same drills on the same oval, over and over and over. Triangles and circles: they are like the separate rails of a train line that run together, side by side, and, despite the narrowing perspective of distance, never intersect.

Ulysses of the Pacific

BEING THE ACCOUNT OF LT. J.S. COWPER, R.N., COMMANDER OF H.M.S. **ANTAEUS,** AND THE SECRET VOYAGE IN SEARCH OF MT PURGATORY IN THE SOUTH PACIFIC DURING THE YEARS 1829–39; GUIDED BY THE SHADES OF DANTE AND VIRGIL, AND THE FLAME OF ULYSSES.

'And he [Antaeus] *shall bear us to the bottom of sin.'*
   Virgil to Dante, *Inf.* xxxi. 102

All hands! the pipe ordered as the last of three bells was silenced by the watch. All hands!

The boatswain stood on the quarterdeck with his right hand curled in an open fist at his lips. From that small cave came the keening whistle of the pipe. As his final three fingers stood in salute then curled down, the whistle sounded low then abruptly high. The effect of movement and sound was similar, although opposite in bias, to the clear-clipped notes of the butcherbird, whose beak points skyward for the high notes, and to the ground for the low (but this was, after all, the southern hemisphere, and all manner of things strove for the opposite). The sustained low to high notes were, after a brief pause, repeated, held aloft, then allowed to fall slowly down the scale to silence.

The urgent order roused the men below deck from dreams and nightmares. Out they fell from rocking hammocks, pulling on woollen sweaters. All hands! the pipe urged, to which the boat-swain added his baritone: 'Heave-ho, heave-ho, lash up and stow. All hands turn out.'

In the gloom of pre-dawn, the shades of men emerged and assembled in orderly rows near the main mast. Their commander, Lieutenant James Stanley Cowper, Royal Navy, stood at the rear of the quarterdeck, facing true east. He had not slept nor moved from his post for two nights and days. He stared along the length of his command and beyond, to where the glory of Easter Sunday smudged the horizon with carnelian.

According to his observations of Hercules and Venus, calibrated with the shipboard chronometers, and methodically reduced in accordance with the tables and formulae in the Nautical Almanac, he placed his command, His Majesty's Ship *Antaeus*, a Titan-class brig currently under full sail, upon the desired latitude and mere minutes of longitude from the meridian of discovery.

Like his late father, Lieutenant Cowper was, apart from a small birthmark on his forehead, physically unremarkable. He began his naval career on Lord Nelson's favourite, H.M.S. *Agamemnon*, the same ship-of-the-line upon which Cowper's late father had served until his death at sea shortly after the siege of Thebes in 1795. Ten years later, he was a teen cadet aboard old Eggs-and-Bacon as she bore down on the French line at Trafalgar. In close fighting under cannonade, he received a remarkable wound to the forehead, in which the stain of his birth was cross-wise splintered. Now, beneath his three-cornered cap and swept-back hair, the features of his face were overwhelmed by the blood-red cross on his brow.

'It is my mark of Cain,' he quipped, hoping to put new acquaintances at ease. 'With it I am seen by God, and thus protected from His hand.' But people were not so easily assuaged, and their eyes ran from his face as from a burning bush or a leper, to rest, at best, at his bearded throat, no higher.

The boatswain glanced at the commander's prominent mark, then lowered his eyes and retreated into the comfort of darkness after having announced, 'All hands present, sir.'

The unsettling effect of the commander's mark was exaggerated by an uncertain phenomenon. A faint flickering aurora of light and shade surrounded the commander, like the penumbra of a solar eclipse such as the crew had recently observed, as if part of his own shadow feared to leave his side. The shady halo spooked the crew, but they could not deny that the master seemed blessed, and had got them out of many a tight encounter. Although they preferred to be stationed at some distance from him, every man without exception would cut off their right hand for the commander, or die in the attempt.

The commander moved forward to address the crew. Mid-step, he halted, turned fully about and cast his penetrating gaze astern across the dim ocean and tilted his head to listen. A stirring sound, carried on the gusts of a strong wind, grew in volume. He perceived the sound of wings beating, the garrulous cry of gulls. It sounded like flying fish … and Sirens. Some of his men began humming the tune that sounded like a funeral psalm, and some others, also recognising it, softly added their voice to the harmonious choir of the wind.

In exitu Israel de Aegypto, domus Iacob de populo barbaro.

The commander too recited the psalm silently … *Mare vidit et fugit* … his head unbowed, his eyes seeking. And he saw … What did he think he saw passing his command?

A phantom ship that skimmed the surface, that neither pushed a wave from her bow nor left a wake behind. A ship piloted by the wings of an angel, and crewed by one hundred human souls bound for Mt Purgatory, and, eventually, the Eternal Paradise: the singing pure, whose lightness would carry them to the summit like an eagle rising on thermal airs; and the chorus of the fortunate penitents, who in death were bound to endure willingly, joyfully, decades or centuries of purifying toil to erase the root of their earthly sins.

Months later in his journal, with no other to dispute his testament, the commander would describe the vision as a flock of giant albatross of a previously undescribed species gliding sonorously on the updraught of the ocean.

A facie Domini mota est terra, a facie Dei Iacob.

The psalm carried past *Antaeus* as both ships bore east towards the dawn. It faded gradually, yet it lingered in the air like a light breeze that barely trembles the main sail.

By habit, the commander said 'Amen', and made the sign of the cross. He moved to the edge of the quarterdeck and took up the railing in his hands. The men gave the hooped insignia on his right sleeve their communal gaze. And conjured now to speak, the commander's tongue flickered within the pit of his open mouth.

'Men, long have we been on this mission of science and discovery. The chart records our wanderings across the peaceful ocean, yet we still have much to accomplish and many leagues to sail afore we can enjoy our furlough. Spare neither a thought for your love in port, nor for the child that knows not the word "father", or your grubby face and rough hands. For what are the pleasures of town and family when compared with the prospects of adventure roving the open seas? That desire and accompanying thrill, it overflows in us all—to discover, and to claim, new lands beyond the horizon for the greater glory of His Majesty.

'My faithful comrades, ye have valiantly endured dozens of jeopardies with me and in all you have proved your worth. Yet afore homeward we can turn, there is now this last vigil to run.

'Under full sail and a favourable westerly, we draw nigh upon the destiny assigned to us by Divine Providence. So now, at sunrise on this glorious Easter Sunday when the Lord Jesus (blessed be

His name) was resurrected to cleanse the earth of sin, I can finally make this confession to you.' He paused and scanned the faces of the men below.

'We sail with secret orders from the Admiralty. Simply put: we sail to claim the Biblical island of Mt Purgatory in the South Pacific.

'And lo, just beyond the rising of the new sun, stands that uncharted isle where no flag of any nation has ever been raised, and save for the poet-prophet Dante,'—who, with the shade of Virgil as his guide, scaled the peak five centuries before in a divine revelation—'upon which no living soul has ever trod.'

At the mention of their deeds, the shadowy darkness about the commander fluttered. The crew responded unconsciously by shifting their weight from one foot to the other.

'During his descent through the circles of Hell,' the commander continued, 'Dante met the tortured soul of Ulysses burning with iniquity. And Ulysses, the sailor king of Ithaca, the sacker of Troy, told him the story of his final voyage beyond the horizon to where his crew feared falling off the earth. The wily Greek had outwitted many gods and sorcerers and titans, but he was powerless beneath the tower of our Lord. Within sight of the mount of our destiny, for his sins the spiralling sea opened wide, and empty words clogged the throat of brave Ulysses as his ship was pulled down into the Underworld with all hands.

'But men, have no fear, for we are divinely sent. When Saint Peter checks your step at the Golden Gate he will ask you: "Pray tell me, what is your name, your country, your glory and your fate?" You can proudly boast that you are British, and your glory was to discover...'

'Land ho!' came the cry from the main topman.

The sailors as one looked up and then turned away from the commander, all straining their eyes to see that which could not yet be seen.

The flickering shadow about the commander flared and separated. Shade moved to one side of the commander while the flame took human shape and jutted out its chest and chin, and clenched its hands like talons around a kill. 'Now!' the flame urged, and the shade of the poets cowered.

'We are at the very threshold of our destiny,' the commander shouted. 'Think now, men, of your duty to king and country. You are born British men. To strive for knowledge and the glory of God. To raise the banner of empire. Long live the King!'

A cheer was raised and suddenly silenced by another call from above. A hushed murmur went through the idlers and yet they still could not see. Only the topmen beheld the glory of dawn.

Mt Purgatory was not manifest in God's initial creation, but like original sin, it was latent within it. When Satan was thrown roaring from the walls of Heaven, the Earthly Paradise bored through the diameter of the planet to escape the tainted angel. Boulders and dirt were pushed down and pushed aside creating the pit of Hell. And boulders and dirt were pushed through the earth's core and pushed upwards, creating the Mount of Purgatory, with the Garden of the Earthly Paradise at its summit, at the portal of Heaven. Many Biblical commentators compress the scale and topography of the peak, reducing to an earth-bound scale that which is of God. But the height of Mt Purgatory is beyond the scope of man's comprehension, beyond sanity and reason. For its rocky base is like that of Mont Blanc, the great peak of the French Alps, yet it rises even more precipitously than the north wall of the Eiger. It is a mighty pillar with sheer rock faces of unscalable rock for tens of thousands of feet into a thick band of clouds and continues to rise, past the point where no cloud forms and no rain falls, and the pillar continues to rise, up and up and up, until its height is equal to the radius of the earth—some four-thousand miles high.

When the golden chariots of the Sun rose above the firmament and the ship advanced over the curve of horizon, the dark pillar of Mt Purgatory reached from the sea to the clouds and cast a column of shadow across the ship that was darker than moonless night. On either side of the strip of shade, the glassy mirror of the ocean shone blindingly and those on watch had to avert their eyes. The mount could be discerned by the shadow it cast, otherwise no details of its topography could be made out, not even with the commander's powerful glass.

Antaeus crept forward in the shadow. A North Sea chill, so at odds with the sub-tropical climate, enveloped the ship. Ice formed on the ropes. The sails spread like frozen lakes.

After several frigid hours, the commander ordered a slight correction to the course to take the ship into the light. As *Antaeus* broached the God-given rays, the ship stopped in a complete calm. There she spent the remaining hours of the day drifting solely on the current as the shadow of the pillar swung around to the south and then stretched out to the east.

As the sun's disc touched the ocean, the pillar resounded with what sounded like squawking gulls. Their screeching coalesced into two choirs, each comprising an untold number of voices that contested in turn for the mercy of the Blessed Virgin and the Lord God of Jacob.

Salve, Regina,
> *Te lucis ante terminum,*
> *rerum Creator, poscimus,*
Mater misericordiae,
> *ut solita clementia,*
> *sis praesul ad custodiam.*
vita, dulcedo, et spes nostra, salve.

Each Compline hymn was sung to its calculated end, half the crew adding their voice to one, half to the other, as was their preference. A final exhalation of downdraught wind from Mt Purgatory briefly filled the sails and brought the hymns to a close ... *Per eumdem Christum Dominum nostrum* ... just as the sudden night fell over the ship like the lid of a coffin ... *Amen.*

*

Through the night the commander maintained his unstinting vigil at the rear of the quarterdeck staring at the mount. The men of the watch took their position apart from him. At the prow, the place on the ship most distant from the commander, a small group gathered, the boatswain among them.

A sweet land breeze blew gently from the pillar. Into the dreams of the somnolent crew it blew the impossible smell of impending success. They dreamed of a landfall on a beach, the king's standard being raised, and hailing his reign with three hearty cheers. They dreamed of scaling the lofty mount and erecting a cairn as a stepping-stone to Heaven. They dreamed of rum and shanties and homeward bound. But to the salts gathered at the prow, the breeze smelled of foreboding; it smelled of the overpowering perfume on an old whore that cannot mask her mouldering flesh; it smelled of pride before the fall, as if Heaven was, in its wrath, luring them to ruin.

'I fear terribly that our doom be near,' one sailor said.

'Aye,' another agreed.

'I cannot sleep. The moment my head hits the hammock I see all the devilish things I done and said...'

'Aye, aye.'

'... and worse, I see my punishment, at the bottom of the pit, plunged to the neck in frozen ice. O 'swain, what meaning is this, this terrifying pillar of rock, the commander's speech?'

'Well...' the boatswain began, trailing off. He did not possess the commander's confidence, no-one on board did, and though he was somewhat educated, he had not the classical and theological education to comprehend the commander's meaning. Before they set sail from Portsmouth, the boatswain had heard rumours in the dock-side taverns. He knew well enough that rumours were not outright lies dressed for the ball, that there was perhaps one quarter-turn of truth in them. But for one quarter-turn he was not going to give the commander up.

'Well,' he began again, 'I heard say many things and his speech was as rousing as any I heard in the closing for battle.' He paused, not knowing how to continue, and turned his head towards the commander at the far end of the brig. The faint glow and shade marked him out against the darkness.

But what could the boatswain really know and understand? For the commander was a master of languages and sciences, of philosophy and theology, and of the 'word of knowledge'. He could have been a professor or a bishop had the circumstances of his youth been different. Fundamentally, the commander believed that the three *canticas* of Dante's *Commedia* were not merely an allegorical tale written to turn people from their sinful ways, to repent and to seek the light of the Lord; he believed that the poet Dante Alighieri was a modern prophet of the Lord, and that his gospel was contained in the verses of *L'Inferno*, *Il Purgatorio*, and *Il Paradiso*. These books he kept bound together with his Holy Bible in his cabin.

And what could the boatswain know of the commander's service and desire?

After the sinking of *Agamemnon* off the River Plate, Cowper was promoted to mate and served on *Menelaus* during the American War. In 1820 he was sent to New Holland to assist Lieutenant Phillip Parker King on his final voyage charting the north-west coastline. Upon his return to England in April 1823, Cowper was given his first command, H.M.S. *Cadmus* in the North Atlantic. When Parker King was selected to lead the Patagonian expedition, the commander forcefully put his case to be assigned, stating that the objectives of the mission should be extended into the Southern Pacific to chart shoals and *vigia* and claim unknown isles, including the Mount of Purgatory. Many within the Admiralty outright scoffed at his proposition, and some, considering him mad, suggested he be relieved of his command. But despite feeling aggrieved at being overlooked for the Patagonian mission, the commander performed his assignments, however laborious, with commendable diligence and zeal. Finally, with all wars over and a new class of surveying brig commissioned for the Age of Exploration, the commander was granted the pursuance of his folly. 'He may return,' one of the admirals surmised, 'or he may be speared by the natives. God willing.'

'One thing I know,' the boatswain finally observed after a long silence, 'I have never known the master to be wrong on any account.'

'Aye,' one sailor ventured, 'but he is mad with it.'

Mad? the boatswain thought, and not for the first time: Aye, mad he may very well be, but he may just be a prophet for our time.

The penumbra about the commander flickered again. Without the daylight of God, the shades of Dante and Virgil slumbered, and the flame of Ulysses became pre-eminent. As the commander stared, he recited cantos from *Purgatorio*, of the landing on the blessed isle, the impending ascension of the poet Statius, and Dante's terror of the final impediment before reaching Paradise: passing through the flaming firewall of lust.

Poi dentro al foco innanzi me si mise,
pregando Stazio che venisse retro,
che pria per lunga strada ci divise.

Si com' fui dentro, in un bogliente vetro
gittato mi sarei per rinfrescarmi,
tant' era ivi lo 'ncendio sanza metro.

'Still your tongue, old man,' the flame whispered, 'or sing the praises of bolder heroes. Sing of the city of Thebes and the wrathful brothers, Eteocles and Polynices; sing of the seven champions of Argos, our fathers; sing of their glory, their fame and their fate.'

The commander's recitation moved seamlessly from the Italian of Dante to the Latin of Statius; from the common speech rendered in hendecasyllabic *terza rima* to dactylic hexameter; from the poets' ascent of Purgatory to the Greek champions entering the plain outside the gates of Thebes.

Lo dolce padre mio, per confortarmi ...
... per et arma et membra iacentum
taetraque congerie sola semianimumque cruorem
cornipedes ipsique ruunt: grauis exterit artus
ungula, sanguineus lauat imber et impedit axes.

'... *the heavy hoof crushes the limbs, and a rain of gore bathes and
clogs the axles. Sweet is it to the heroes to go by such a road* ... Ah,' the
flame of Ulysses sighed and flickered, stamping out each line with
his foot in time. And conjured by the song, Capaneus, perhaps the
greatest of those seven Greek champions, slapped Ulysses on the
back and the two flames clasped forearms. Ulysses spat a flaming
gob overboard, then made ready for another arm wrestle.

*

By dawn on Easter Monday, *Antaeus* had drifted with her crew of
living souls within miles of the pillar that rose impossibly above
the small ship like a mountain ash tree above an ant. The pillar, so
silent during the night, suddenly thundered and shook violently,
as if a large boulder had been rolled aside. The men of the watch
looked up in alarm. A dread gripped them, as it grips the thief
or murderer about to be crucified. As one they raised their arms
above their heads for protection. They expected a crushing hail of
rocks, the wrath of angels. Instead, the mount erupted in song:
  Gloria!
The crew stood stupefied.
  Gloria in excelcis ... They raised their arms to shoulder height
... *in excelcis Deo* ... and pressed their palms together at their
hearts and bowed.
  Gloria! Gloria in excelcis Deo.
And too suddenly, the glorious rocky chorus closed ... *Amen* ...
and the crew, each having made of their body a large sign of the
cross, returned to their tasks. But the silence of Mt Purgatory was

brief, and the sad refrain of day was taken up by thousands of souls competing for recognition and repentance.

Miserere mei, Deus: secundum magnam misericordiam tuam.

The voices of the sorry souls longing for the light of God flew from the mighty pillar on the wings of seabirds that now circled the ship.

The high soloing of sopranos, grounded by the blend of altos and tenors and baritones and bass, acted like a cleansing balm on the stained souls of the sailors. Wave upon wave, the psalm washed over them, from high to low, with melancholy, with pleading, with a promise.

Amplius lava me ab iniquitate mea: et a peccato meo munda me.

The lamentation caused some of the sailors to fall to their knees, to weep and pray for the salvation of their immortal souls.

''Swain,' the commander called, 'stopper the men's ears with wax and get some chain to bind me to the mizzen-mast. And 'swain, no matter what I say, do not release my bindings until we have made ready for shore. Go.'

The general order was piped and passed, and the instructions were hurriedly carried out. The commander, his ears unstoppered, was bound like a Titan, five times around his chest down to his waist, his arms pinned and his hands out of sight behind; the chain continued encircling him to his ankles. The lament continued, unceasing.

Tibi soli peccavi, et malum coram te feci: ut justificeris in sermonibus tuis, et vincas cum judicaris.

The now deaf crew bent to their task. *Antaeus* circled the mount anti-clockwise. With the glass, the mate searched for a safe harbour or a bay wherein to make a landing but there appeared only the vertical ramparts of a rock fortress that blocked out half the sky, and the ceaseless sets of waves that pounded them. But as they completed their circumnavigation, the mate espied a narrow spit and a reedy beach that might serve as a landing place on the eastern shore. He brought the ship around to within an easy row and silently signalled the preparation of the boats for a landing.

At the bow, soundings were taken for the anchor but the chain ran out to the bitter end without grounding. The mate informed the commander that the ship would have to maintain sail as there was no anchorage. The commander assented with a nod, which the mate passed on to the boatswain, who stood at attention and piped the general order then boomed: 'Lower the boats!'

For the crew, the 'swain's pipe and call broke the intimate silence of their beating hearts, but for the commander, the *Miserere* continued without relief.

Ecce enim in iniquitatibus conceptus sum: et in peccatis concepit me mater mea.

After the boatswain's *fortissimo* baritone faded on the breeze, another sound emerged, a sound that only the commander could hear. A dangerous sound—of water churning, of waves crashing—of barely submerged rocks; a shoal or reef. The commander looked every way for the source of danger. All about, the sea was as still as oil. Yet the ominous churning continued.

'Release me now,' the commander called. ''Swain, unbind these chains.' The commander wrestled with his bindings without effect.

Even if he had heard the commander shouting, the boatswain would not have paid heed. He continued overseeing the preparations for a landing, when from the pillar a squall suddenly blew. At the turbulent union of Paradise and Earth, where the tongue of the fresh waters of the River of Oblivion run into salt, the sea churned with whirlpools and eddies and *Antaeus* was captured as if in liquid ice. She was twisted and spun anti-clockwise. Time rushed backwards. And as she spun a gale dashed violently athwartships. The sails wrenched. The swollen masts shrieked.

'Drop the sails!' the commander shouted, still bound. 'Drop the sails!'

Aware of the danger even without hearing the order, the men clambered with much difficulty up the rigging of the spinning ship. The sails were cut clear, but still the brig was assailed, as pleased Another.

Ne proiicias me a facie tua: et spiritum sanctum tuum ne auferas a me.

And so beleaguered, the commander raised his only weapon, his voice, to Heaven. But his motivation was neither pious nor subservient. He shook with boastful pride like the Greek hero Capaneus when he stood atop the ramparts of Thebes, and the minor gods trembled as towering Capaneus challenged almighty Zeus, the Thunderer, to single combat. The commander's shades likewise trembled, but the flame about him grew terrifyingly as if he stood within his own pyre.

'It is I, O Lord,' he shouted, 'he who bears Your unmistakable stain.' The damned cross on his forehead throbbed. 'I am borne by the placid giant *Antaeus* that ne'er brooked any quarrel with You, yet still it bears me to the very base of sin, and repentance. In praise of You, we have raised Your bloody banners in holy war against the heathen in Palestine and Europe, and against the heretics of England and Ireland. And now I bear the flag of our holy empire to claim the soil of Your Earthly Paradise for Your most humble and loyal servant, our king.'

Libera me de sanguinibus, Deus, Deus salutis meae: et exsultabit lingua mea justitiam tuam.

At this the heavens shook and a trident-shaped lightning bolt struck the three mast tops. The lightning rods (the work not of gods but of men) diffused the strikes. The timbers failed to shatter or burst. But the boy atop the main mast was tossed from his box. For a brief moment the boy stood on solid air. In that moment he was between being master and being mastered. Then he fell, like Capaneus fell, like we all will fall: wondering. The sea fled from his terrifying shadow then closed over him.

The circling gulls flew off. Lice sloughed off the sailors like snake skins. Rats emerged from below and leapt overboard, preferring their fear of drowning while swimming over certain death on the ship.

'We are doomed,' several of the crew cried.

Quoniam si voluisses sacrificium, dedissem utique: holocaustis non delectaberis.

They got down on their knees. They raised their palms and faces to the sky and recited the final prayers of a sailor:

Mother of Carthage, I return my oar.
I sleep; presently I row again.
O Lord, judge me not as a god, but as a man
whom the Ocean has broken.

In the darkened church of the commander's mind, a priest moved about slowly, diligently, extinguishing the lighted candles one by one with a long-handled snuff, their smoke rising briefly, until there was only one flame remaining, hidden from view. The priest put down the snuffer and departed from the muted light.

In a smothering roar of elemental wind and water, the brig spun three times more. And on the fourth, the poop rose and the prow dipped. Into the churning water the brig was sucked down. Sucked down and rolled over. Water ripped across the drowned decks. And then, like an iceberg righting itself after breaking free of an ice-shelf, *Antaeus* lifted her prow from the icy deep. Her unbroken fingers and naked decks rose into the air as the wounded sea healed over.

Tunc acceptabis sacrificium justitiae, oblationes, et holocausta: ...

The wind abated, the sea relented; *calando, ritmico*. On the dissipating waves and eddies, unable to be crushed, *Antaeus* bobbed like a dry cork.

... tunc imponent super altare tuum vitulos.

The final note of the psalm, the fallen B flat, sung a *nessuna cosa* by the sopranos, restored a hushed calm. And the ship, save for the one whose pride is unconquerable, had been cleared—had been cleared of all hands.

The hangman and the hanged man

Hanging is a fine art and not a mechanical trade. Is not a man an artist who can painlessly and without brutality despatch another man?

Charles Duff, *A Handbook on Hanging*

I come to prepare him & he be ready. It be a little after 9 in the morn & he just been brung up to the last room. After this no more room, no more cell. If I been a godly man then I might say diffrnt but no god can love him. Hair falls to the bluestone floor, long dark hair from his beard & head. I sharpn the razor & think maybe I can end this early but I be wantin to do my first job well. Today Im the ringer & I run him over like a prize ram. His skull come up good & shiny. I dont leave no nicks.

I done the messurmnts & Mister Doctor he help me, my sums not bein good. The culprit he says must be weighd evryday so it can be done proper, not messy. He showd me this book he keeps writ all fancy with pictures of knots & bones. I grunt at the knots, paw at the pages.

The Doctor be very particlar that it not be botchd. He dont want no bruises or cuts. No chokin or decapitayshun. He say it be like crackin a whip. I think it be like pullin a black snake from the grass & crackin its neck. A quick death makes good eatin after, the flesh be sweet & tasty.

The Sheriff brung me the new Russian hemp rope 'for treatmnt' he say. It need to be drownd in hot water then stretchd by hangin a 28-pound sack of lead shot from it. The rope be heavy, too thick to lasso a horse with. It be more like them ropes from my sailor days, hoistin the heavy canvas sails, or tied to the end of the anchor chain.

When the Doctor aint lookin I pocket his book. He mark a page, say it very importnt. I rip it out. I try to be neat.

> The length of the drop may usually be calculated by employing the following method:
>
> Length of drop (feet) = 840 / weight of the culprit in his clothing (pounds)
>
> The result gives the length of the drop in feet, but no drop should exceed eight feet. Thus a person whose clothed weight is 140 pounds would require a drop of six feet. The table can be used on this basis up to 210 pounds.
>
> When for any special reason, such as a diseased condition of the neck of the culprit, the Governor and Doctor think that there should be a departure from this table, they may inform the executioner, and advise him as to the length of the drop which should be given in that particular case.

I know he carry the black card in his leg iron. The sick judge in scarlet finery & black cap he give it him two week ago. That judge he be a great fortune teller the bods say & they dont be liars. They say his ma offerd the judge the full use of her shebeen but the judge say she is gone dry & aint worth his spit.

Last night I get the cell next him. I sleep like a baby but he be wakin me with cursin & wailin. The priest be with him. The priest say 'God be with you' but he still be screamin 'There be no god in what I seen.' I listen close when he tell:

Carried on my grey mare bolting through the steep scrub of the range, the horse bucks as a king brown snake rears up to strike and thrown into the air upside down my foot is caught in a noose suspended from a red ironbark, my hands are bound in the green-hide whip, the snake coils around my leg & down my trousers while I swing treading on the blue. Thick humus of rusted leaf & twig & nuts form my sky, ants populate the strange new limb & kookaburras peck at flesh exposing the worms & slugs hidden in my underbelly. Blood pools in my head, the veins in my temples bulge & leeches sensing my heat rise from the leaves & attach to my scalp giving me a bloody crown.

I like the feel of his shiny bald skull. I be quick, not be suspishus. But I aint felt anuvr for longer than my life is worth. It be so smooth. I can feel the heat risin from the roundness. I take speshl attenshun to the small dips & lumps, run my finger along the scar above his right ear. It be not less than five inches I can tell even with my eyes closd.

I seen people hangd before & I hear many tales. If it be done real good then the hangd man do get some pleasure. When I were young they strung em up outside the town hall. There was three of em, murdrers, & a large crowd turn up, many women too, howlin & bawlin. The murdrers was brought out naked & taken to a platform beneath a large red gum. When they dropd they all crackd a stiffy like they was havin a scrape with the tarts on Satdy night then the bawlers in the front rows got an eyeful.

I musta been fifteen, not even clapd hands on a girl. It were quite an educayshun.

I wanna make him scrape with me. When I pull the lever it be his cock in my hand. When he drop I be ready to take his last rites.

Remind me of what I hear sung in the streets of Ballarat befor I been put in here. I hear some of the fellas hummin it whenevr he go past.

> There be a man named Kelly
> With a fire in his belly
> From his little shotgun
> The troopers they run
> To the waitin arms of Kelly
>
> He have a brother calld Dan
> Whos in love with anuvr man
> He say 'Dan dont you do
> What Id never do
> Put ya penny in anuvr mans can'

He get a visit from the Guvners son. He like tellin tales from the old country to the lad, he bein a gumsucker. His Ma teach him about Cuchulainn, a warrior boy-king. It be his fayvrit. At fourteen he be ridin trick horses & shootin targets at a gallop. He ride straight down the side of ravines so steep no man on foot dare follow, his grey mare & him have a speshl bond. He can kill one hundred men in single combat there be no deadlyr with gun or fist. True, he wear the green ring of the first man he killd.

But he be bound by his taboos. If he break em he become mortal.

No food offerd can he refuse but he not be allowd to eat dog, so he carnt refuse the lady of the hotel who servd up a plate of dingo stew. He ate evry bit of gristle & suckd the marrow from the bone, felt his power weakn. & he must trust anyone wingd or crippld so he let that dog Curnow go & raise the alarm.

When the hotel blazd at dawn he came at em outta the fog & smoke in his battle armour poundin his pistol butt on his iron neck, howlin like a bunyip. They outnumbrd him more than an outsider at the local races but he held em off for most the day. Bullets raind on him & dentd his iron bruisin him all over. His grey mare nuzzld him but he carnt grab the reins & lift his hundred-twenty pound armour in the stirrup. His legs be riddld with bullets. So he lashd hisself to a granite tor with his leather whip so he defy his enemy & die on his feet.

Him he tell it that way. But I hear diffrnt.

I hear he be rolld on the ground, the shotgun blasts in his legs fellin him like an ironbark to be split up for fence posts. Two men it take to lift off the iron helmet. His bloody beard & puffy face make him barely recognisabl.

It be only five or six steps but he shuffl along, take him forty-nine. I watch him close & hear the Doctor whisper oer my shoulder, he be particlar to countin. His arms be piniond with leather belt already cos I done that. His face be very pale like he seein his dead da or somethin on the platform.

I can feel the Doctors eyes & hands followin mine. This bein my first time & with such an importnt man, he want me do it good. The large slipknot go right behind the ear like he showd me. I pull it tight. This man he have nothin to say.

Today I be write in the papers. E-l-i-j-a-h U-p-j-o-h-n. Do somethin no wombat-arsd copper ever done. Today it be legal. Aint no court convict me this murdr.

Encounter at Kalayakapi c.1871

Ants transform the red dirt into broad avenues that shimmer with their relentless movement like heat haze on tar. Flies mass on the unexpected feast—to maggotise, to multiply. The native cats, sated on the guts, juicy eyes, gristly ears, and meagre flesh, sleep through the interminable summer heat, leaving the carcass to improve in the outdoor oven. The animal is large, almost devoid of hair. The body is pitched forward into a rough sort of burrow, an unfinished excavation in the dry creek bed. Most of the nails on its front paws have been pulled off; the tips are bloodied stumps.

—There's water three hundred yards up the creek, Mr Gray. A native well. Plenty of native tracks leading to it. We'll need to dig it out for all of the horses to water.

—Well done, Mr Whytte. Lead on. We'll make camp there.

Down by the soakage the two men dismount. After two days without water, the horses are nearly knocked up. While Mr Whytte wearily unloads the distraught pack-horses, Mr Gray surveys the landscape.

The hunting fires of the natives burn a few miles to the south. The thick, black smoke from the burning spinifex hurtles skyward like souls eager to reach heaven. Hundreds of kite-hawks circle low over the flames, ready to grab a lizard, a bilby or a singed kangaroo before the native spears and nulla nullas intervene.

—What kind of world is this? he mutters. Fire. The native is always burning. Even on these furnace days when the stirrup irons brand the horse's belly and the bit scalds its tongue. He will burn this country black and disappear in the ash.

Mr Gray removes his wide-brimmed felt hat, bows his head forward slightly to mop his brow on the sodden shirtsleeve of his crooked arm. Hundreds of flies, stirred from his back by the movement, rise into a halo around his unprotected head. He swats lethargically, knowing they will soon resettle on his sweat-soaked back. He replaces the hat and refocuses his attention. He turns where he stands and bellows to his companion.

—There's good feed here for the horses, Mr Whytte. No need for the hobbles tonight.

The old bearded men sit in agitated council between two fires within a cleared patch of spinifex. Their dogs lie sphinx-like on the outer perimeter, sniffing at the darkness. Several young warriors hunting *malu* and *kalaya*, red kangaroo and emu, came across something disturbing earlier in the day and had run in alarm back to their camp.

The voices of the old men circle in turn around the fire-lit mob.

—They have six legs but no toes, two heads, stand as high as a spear, split into spirit men and thunder feet.

—They have tracks we have never seen before, do not know how to make.

—They drink all of our *kapi*, don't leave any for us, for *malu*, for *kalaya*.

—They are come from out of the earth, as we all have.

—Their arms are as white as quartz, as white as *pilpira*, the ghost gum that the possums live in. They must be ghosts of the old people.

—They are our *kurun-kurunpa*. They should sit down over there.

—They haven't asked for permission to be on our country.

—They should talk to us.

—What are we being punished for that these *kurun-kurunpa*, these *walypala* have come here?

—Maybe that cheeky mob from the stone country sent them. Their *kadaitja* are very powerful.

The spinifex fires and circling *paningka* kite-hawks point to the hunting natives, just as surely as the gunshot blasts echoing down the range give away the explorers, the *walypala*. Galahs screech and launch from *apara* red gums. The cobalt sky transforms into alternating pink and grey flashes as the birds call and whirl about, this way and that. Another blast echoes along the sandstone cliffs like a thundering chorus of drums, rolling repeatedly back and forth for almost a minute. Downy feathers slowly fall through the gnarled branches. The explorers have tried roasting and frying pink cockatoo and parakeet, but it is only as a stew that the birds become remotely palatable. But what else is there to eat? They are out of salt, their pork barrels are rancid. They endure on leathery strips of smoked horsemeat that make their teeth wobble and their gums bleed, and a ball of boiled flour, no more.

Tjilpi, a learned old greybeard, gives instruction to the new initiates. The boys, although still young, are now young men, and having learnt some of the ways of the women, now begin to learn the responsibilities of a man, a hunter.

—*Kuka kalaya* came through here. Walking. Male. One year old. Stopped here and turned east. Another *kalaya* coming from south of east. Also male. Four years old. Seven little *akalpa* following. One of them a bit slower. He'll be tucker for *paningka* soon. Single *kalaya* wanted to steal the trailing *akalpa*. Father *kalaya*, he chased him away. Yesterday. Just after sunrise.

The hunting mob leave the *tjina* of the father, leave him to raise his little ones, follow the *tjina* of the young male *kalaya* across the claypan to *kurku*, the mulga scrub.

—*Malu* been sleeping there, *tjilpi* points out. He sleeps there most days. *Kalaya* woke him up. *Malu* hopped and walked slowly away from the sun. *Kalaya* went the opposite way for a bit, scratched about for some tucker then went on.

A faint glint in the sand about ten steps away catches the eye of *tjilpi*. Crescent-shaped tracks leading east show up beside a small metallic cylinder the colour of corkwood flowers.

—*Walypala*, *tjilpi* says to himself. Yesterday. Before midday.

The old man turns back to the initiates to continue the lesson.

—We sweep our tracks so kalaya can't follow us, won't know we have been following him. We make ourselves invisible so the kadaitja man, that magician-assassin, cannot make his sickness magic on us either. But the walypala, he must have strong powers. He's not scared of kadaitja. He leaves bits of himself everywhere: his tjina in the sand, his shit on the surface like a dog marking his territory, letting the bitches know he's ready to rut. He scatters his kill liberally and wastes the best meat, the fatty meat from the malu tail.

After several days of fruitless searching and false leads, the explorers eventually find another native well in a red-gum creek. Tired and thirsty from the long hot days and scant rations, they set up camp only yards from the water beneath the tree's ample shade. They had soon drawn several full buckets for their horses to drink.

During their five-day stay beside the well, no kangaroos or natives were able to visit it, the most reliable source of water for many days walk in any direction. The *walypala* and their horses ran it dry. The zebra finches were forced to drink the pungent, drying mud. The natives and their fires had already moved on.

The meat from the last of their packhorses cures in the makeshift smokehouse after an awful day of butchery. Flies pulse over the fleshy titbits on the ground outside. Mr Whytte kicks dust over the writhing mass and curses at the stench. He enters the flimsy tent and adds an armful of green leaves and branches to the fire beneath the curing racks.

—I'm glad this is the last one, he mutters to no-one.

For the next three days Mr Whytte will be the barbarous attendant to his flesh-eating needs, tending the fire and smoke, turning the strips of muscle, rotating them among the different levels to encourage even drying. In the smokehouse, Mr Whytte is tortured by the smoke stinging his weeping eyes; he is tortured by the flies creeping over his face and into his ears and mouth; he is tortured by the ants in their millions trying to carry away his best work yet; and he is reminded of his own precarious mortal existence by the stench of death that no amount of bathing and scrubbing can remove.

Resting in the oppressive late-afternoon heat beneath a river red gum, Mr Gray reflects on the untidy appearance of eucalypts. Their habit, their form, their mottled colour and their tendency to silently shed limbs on still days are repulsively foreign, so unlike a tall poplar, a majestic pine, a towering elm, or a grand and shady oak.

He closes his eyes and thinks longingly of home. The gentle breeze stiffens and the dull grey-green lanceolate leaves wave up and down like a lady's handkerchief signalling from a horse-drawn carriage in Bath, or even, God forbid, the colonial equivalent, Melbourne. The agitated branchlets shake the lerp scale from the leaves. It falls in a shower of sugary snow, coating his face, beard and body. Like a slow-motion thorny devil on a sugar-ant trail, his unmoving mouth pushes out a pointed tongue, captures a sweet morsel and draws it in. The sweet waxy drop reminds him of the comforts of childhood, encased in warm blankets, sucking on a honey-dipped dummy.

Once, long ago, this old gum shared its shade and secrets with the Munga Munga women, and in return, the tiny women left their children on the burls and boughs where they were lulled to sleep by the slow murmurings of the tree. The women went west to fill their coolamons with *kuraltja* and *kumpurarpa*, maybe get a goanna along the way. They went west and kept on going.

When the children awoke, alone and hungry, they suckled from the nectar-rich flowers and sugar-coated leaves of *apara*, their aunty.

Now they creep up to Mr Gray, sleeping where their mothers abandoned them. They tug lightly on his beard; he involuntarily swats a fly away. They remove his hat and place it on a high branch; the leader does not flinch. They sit on his leg, remove his right boot and reel at the stench released; the *walypala's* toes wiggle, tempting the crows to strike.

Tjilpi lays down his spears in the cover of the bushes and steps forward into the clearing. His companions, two well-proportioned young men, hold their ground a few paces behind. Caught unawares, Mr Gray turns from the fire and gasps. Mr Whytte thinks about making for the gun, thinks better of it. The two warriors appear relaxed, but their eyes are fixed on the *walypala*. They hold their spears firmly.

Tjilpi steps forward. This is his country. He has waited too long for the *walpalya* to show due respect for the land and its custodians. He walks up to Mr Gray. *Tjilpi* smiles, revealing a stack of white teeth, stark against the dark skin. He reaches for Mr Gray's beard and strokes it tenderly. He pats him on the chest, all the while smiling.

Mr Gray's initial fear of being speared recedes, and he surprises himself by reaching out to the old man and fondling his beard. The old man chuckles. He says something and the young men advance. Mr Gray's hand freezes, still clutching the old man's beard. The old man laughs again at the frightened eyes staring at him. One of the young men holds a large bird, somewhat like a goose, and he gives this to the old man who presents it to Mr Gray.

Mr Gray holds the dead bird as *tjilpi* gives a speech. He nods respectfully, as if he understands and fully agrees with what the old man is telling him. What fortune, he thinks, the welcome passport for our progress through these parts.

Tjilpi seems pleased with the meeting. He pinches Mr Gray on the cheek and laughs. The young warriors smile, and on the verge of retreating to the scrub, they each quickly squeeze Mr Gray's cheek, daring themselves to touch the ghost standing before them.

The silent, invisible *tjina* are everywhere around the disorganised camp. Mr Gray, wrapped up tight in his blanket like a corpse, snores lightly. Ants crawl all over his body seeking food, but he is oblivious to their small pincers.

Mr Whytte is not so fortunate. He has become more insomniac, unable to find a place to sleep free of the black trails of ants. Wherever he drops they spew from their volcanic slits to crawl into his clothing and nip and tear at his flesh. He scratches and howls, jumps up and down, tries to rip the thin mortal layer from his bones. The *kadaitja*, sitting in the darkness outside the circle of light of the small camp-fire, rises and noiselessly floats away on emu-feathered feet, leaving no footprints. Mr Gray does not stir.

The horses hobble off during the night in search of feed and water. Dawn reveals the explorers in the same repose as when the setting sun drew down the blanket of night: propped against the knobbly trunk of a lone coolibah. Their heads hang forward— heavy weights: too heavy for their necks to hold up, too heavy to balance a hat. They do not move. Not even when the negligible shade of the straggly tree withdraws and they are plunged into the intense burning of full sun. They could be sleeping, so at rest do they appear. Or they could be … no, not yet. Their shirts flutter slightly, in time with their slow, shallow breath.

—Those fellas, they've gone mad, poorfellas. They walk everywhere. *Tjina* going every way. Why don't they listen? I told them they are not welcome here right now, take this bird and eat well because you gotta leave. We've got ceremony business. Lots of people coming. I told them which way to go, where they can get water, not north, nothing that way, but they gotta go more east. But they go north and west, wrong way, into that wide thicket of *kurku*, poorfellas.

Tjilpi shakes his head with sad concern.

—Poor *walypala*. They must have blind eyes. Don't they know the *tjurkupa*? Everything is written for them to read: in the trees, the rocks, the sky, even in the ants. They can't see our *tjina, mitura wanani.*

A solitary native carrying his spears enters the creek bed. To foreign eyes this creek looks like any other for hundreds of miles around, this section interchangeable with countless others along its length. But each metre and tree along the length of every creek is unique, and the native recognises this place. It is *Kalayakapi*, emu *tjurkupa*, his mother's father's country. Nearby along the easterly pad, a mob of stately desert oaks whisper to each other beneath the crest of a cayenne pepper–coloured sand ridge.

He is thirsty, but still some distance from the next waterhole, a soakage called *Kalayapiti*. He seeks out the large *apara* on the opposite bank, upstream a little way from the rotting *kuka*, the *walypala*. A green flash of budgerigars shrieks and darts through the lower branches of the grand gum.

Whispering to the tree, his mother, he picks up several hollow tubes of bark and forms them into a long straw. He inserts one end into a small orifice in the tree's belly, sups the rainwater held secretly inside. With great care he removes the tubes and places them at his feet, ready for the next person to use, then continues his journey, softly singing the country into being.

At Gallery cV3

W e are led to a side room off the foyer and wordlessly instructed to sit. More people are led in to the vacant seats. When the last is occupied, the room is darkened.

On the screen, a well-groomed young couple, smiling and laughing, stop in front of the gallery. They take a selfie or two. She posts to Facebook while he tweets. They skip inside with waves and hellos. The gallery assistant points to a sign above the door leading from the foyer into the gallery: PHOTOGRAPHY NOT PERMITTED. The couple smile and nod and walk through. At the first exhibit, she raises her phone to shoot. Her partner stands beside and with his back to her, poised to take a selfie of them while she takes a photo of the art. There is the sound of two camera shutters opening and closing. Then there is the sight and sound of the two young bodies crumpling to the floor, their phones vibrating across the polished cement like netted fish on the deck of a boat. The camera pans across to a silencer on a handgun held by a security guard, his other hand pointing up to the sign behind him. Zoom in on the sign. And keep zooming even after the illegible small print is revealed.

Silent Awe

What the —, my partner begins to say. She is shushed by a gallery attendant who turns on her with a finger raised to her closed lips. My partner looks at me and raises her eyes. As she leads me across the bare room we pass a grimacing art patron, right arm chicken-winged behind their back, being escorted from the room through a side door.

We stop in the exact centre of the room where a small square mat silently declares

You are at
the centre
of the room.

From this focal point we observe. The walls, the ceiling, the floor are a uniform gloss white, without any adornment or display. Around the room art patrons stand like statues. Their arms are crossed over their chests or held behind their backs. Their faces exhibit reverence and silent rapture. They could be part of an installation. The room is quieter than a library, quieter than a mortuary.

What is this, my partner whispers into my ear so softly that I barely hear her, some kind of church?

A gallery attendant, one finger across his lips, thrusts a card at my partner. SECOND WARNING. She turns it over: WILL YOU BE PLEASE BE QUIET.

Jonah

A gallery attendant wearing white shoes and pants and a green t-shirt with NEXT cV3 written in white across the chest indicates the way to the next room. We plunge through the overlapping folds of heavy white curtains into absolute dark. My arms reach out automatically to touch something, a wall, someone, anything, to latch on to. We shuffle forward, feeling our way with our toes and fingertips. A passage leads off to the right. I try to recall the rule for negotiating labyrinths. Is it to always take the right path?

We turn. Shuffle on. The way seems to descend. Turn right again. Further down. What minotaur lurks at the centre of this maze? We turn right a third time. The way is now upslope. I feel a series of soft curtains then emerge from the belly of the whale into overwhelming light.

Random selection

There are seven curtained-off rooms on each side. My partner enters the third right. I get sixth left. There is a cushioned seat, an interactive computer screen. I press the green button and the rules are silently displayed one by one on the screen. Am I ready to begin? the screen asks.

I get dealt seven lettered tiles. The seconds slide away. The ten-second warning beeps. I move the word onto the Scrabble board. It's not much, but it is a start, the beginning of a fable.

I replace the used tiles. Another minute passes, another word is added to the board, more tiles replace used tiles. And this goes on until there are seven words on the board. My random Scrabble poem.

I wonder if anyone has been able to use all 49 letters. I wonder what the highest possible poem score is. My partner comes out smiling as she receives a message with the text of her poem.

This is all I manage: 54 points, less 21 for the five unusable tiles—A_1, I_1, I_1, Q_{10}, X_8—remaining on the rack. Once – spins – yore – raid – dig – gay.

Fur ball

When it is our turn, gallery attendants lead us by the arm to separate soundproof pods into which we step and sit, arms on the armrest. A helmet comprising 360-degree panoramic virtual reality goggles and surround-sound speakers is fitted and clipped. Stimulating electrodes are pegged to index fingers. Forearms are velcroed to the armrest. The pod lid closes.

There is vision, sound and sensation. If I turn or lift my head then the view alters, but it is like looking out of a gun turret. The lack of peripheral vision is disorienting.

A voice blabs on. Some stream of consciousness monologue. I cannot get past the bit where the artist (or is it a voice actor substituting for the artist?) describes his artistic mission using a clumsy mixed metaphor. I try to take off the audio-visual helmet but I can't lift my arms. I forgot the damn straps. I am held captive until the artist can cough up the fur ball gagged in his throat.

What is it with all this art-wank? Since when did it become a pre-requisite for contemporary artists to frontload their artwork, to explain their personal symbols and metaphors? If the artwork is incomprehensible without such exposition, then hasn't it, even in a small way, failed?

What is required?

A title. A provocation.

The artist has an intention. They attempt to realise their intention in form. It is then for others to interpret. Artists can be surprised or stimulated by the interpretations of their artworks, but they should never be disappointed. What they get is the anticipated by-product of what they have produced. And since everybody's experience of the world is unique, even ever-so-slightly, then just one artwork can be transformed into a thousand-headed buddha, each face with a different facet.

I could go on, but the artist's or voice actor's monologue, without me noticing, has already ceased. The pod door is open.

Creation

Before the opening of this exhibition the four walls of the room were whitewashed. At the very centre of the white wall opposite the doorway, a single black square, one inch by one inch, was placed. This small black square acts as both a catalyst and an invitation. The gallery attendant explains all of this before we are allowed to enter the room.

Just inside the room, two white vending machines, one on each side of the doorway, stand guard. Insert coin here. Two dollars ejects a four-by-three sheet of one-inch square black stickers. And an invoice for the donation—please retain for tax purposes. The sound of creation is the metallic scrape and crash of coins pushed through slots and falling into a burgeoning pit of profit.

Who is the artist here? my partner asks.

I look for a name on the wall, turn my sheet of black stickers over. It says JAC.

Everyone wants to be an artist for a moment, to participate in the creation of this ever-evolving installation. Black squares are covering white space. Black squares are creating new shapes. Black squares are overlaying black squares.

Some artist is making a lot of money out of this idea, my partner observes. They have as much influence over this piece of art as a listless god.

After placing their black squares, people move on to the next room. They soon return and purchase more stickers and place these on the wall. I give my remaining squares to my partner to place and go to the next room. The room seems smaller than that next-door, but of the exact same proportions. Projected on the four walls by four separate projectors mounted from the ceiling are videos made from time-lapse images of the corresponding four walls of creation next door. They loop through.

There is the initial moment of creation, where a single black dot appears at the centre of unanimous white. Then black dots appear randomly like freckles. They coalesce to form masses of blackness. They spread. They spot the side walls, the back wall, like a pox, a plague.

How long will it take until the room is more black than white? How long until the small dark squares move to the floor, the ceiling? How long until the room is as dark as the belly of a whale? Until it spreads to other rooms?

I notice some black squares on my partner's top when she comes into the video room just as creation loops back to the whiteout beginning and recommences.

Apologia

How much longer? my partner asks. We have been in the gallery for hours now.

There is no way of telling, I say.

We emerge from a long narrow passage into a double room. In the middle of each half of the room, two large columns or pillars slowly rotate. The columns are not circular; their bases and capitals are squat cylinders, but their tall shafts are triangular prisms—comprised of three panels, all of the same dimensions, they form in cross-section an equilateral triangle. A rectangular wing extends from the vertices of each triangular prism, blinkering the panels in such a way that, no matter where you stand in the room, only one panel of each rotating triptych can be seen at any one time.

The three panels of one pillar are painted a pinkish-white, skin white. The other is almost black, glossy like wet skin. I stand there for a time between the two twirling columns to take in what each triptych displays. On the black pillar, one panel has a skin-coloured stencil plastered across the middle with the word Sᴏʀʀʏ cut out. The title at the base states Dᴜʀɪɴɢ. The other two panels appear to be the same, completely unadorned, just near-black, with one named Bᴇꜰᴏʀᴇ the other, Aꜰᴛᴇʀ. It is only after looking at the latter panel for some time that a faint outline develops, similar to the image-burn after staring at a yantra or mandala, which appears to repeat the word 'sorry'.

The skin-white triptych is similarly organised with before, during and after panels. The stencil is near-black. The word: Sʜᴀᴍᴇ

I walk around one of the columns, keeping in time with its rotation, such that despite our movement, our position relative to each other remains fixed. In this way I can stay forever in denial, in a time before shame, before any word was necessary. I can allow time to catch up with me and continually apologise, saying sorry–sorry–sorry like a mantra, over and over and over. And then there is the time after, when an apology, any apology, is like a dream woken from too soon to recall.

The outrage of Raymond Carver

for GL

Tuesday 8 July 1980, 10:13am
Gordon.

Gordon, Christ. I've been calling for hours.

Yeah, yeah. Look, Gordon, I read the edit … yes … no … no Gordon, just let me… Please, let me explain. I read the edit, yes. Yesterday. Then I guess I walked out of the house. I walked out of the house and got in the car and drove. Just drove. I drove around town all afternoon. I don't know where I got to, I just kept on driving. I didn't notice anything except for every drug store I drove past. I slowed down for nothing but those drug stores. My head spun slowly as I cruised past seeing people go in and come out, in and out, so many people going in and coming out of those drug stores. But I kept driving. Got so I couldn't read the dials on the dash. I kept on driving until some guy pulled up beside me at a red light and wound down his side window and shouted at me 'You trying to kill someone or what?' He sped off when the lights changed. I sat there, the engine humming, wondering what to do.

I flicked on the headlights and saw a gun store across the road. So now here I am, at home, all on my lonesome in the dining nook. My right hand is on the formica in front of me, fingers spread, forming a triangle on the table with two objects. A Smith and Wesson, loaded. A fifth of Four Roses, seal cracked. By God, Gordon, I haven't touched a drop in three years, not since that last episode, you know that, but there's no-one else around and I need to hold something and I don't know which one it's going to be.

You've got some balls, Gordon, no doubt about it, you're a fucking genius. But I'm at my limit here. This is what your fucking genius has driven me to. Guns and whiskey. I have half a mind to jump in the car and drive down to your office now and—BLAM!— Did you hear that? The next bullet is yours.

Shocked! To say I'm shocked is a fucking understatement. I feel like I have gone to the barber for a shave and trim and when he lifts the mirror for me to inspect I see I've been scalped! So no, I don't think I'm over-reacting. This is not a midday soap. We aren't some cheap-ass characters in a goddamn story.

I know, I know, I should have looked at this earlier, but you know how much I value your critical eye. We go back a long ways, Gordon. I trust you. And besides, these stories are not raw drafts. Some of them you have edited before. And they have all been, or soon will be, published in journals or by small press. So I am shocked to my core to see them so abusively treated. Why didn't you call me? Why not just call me? You know: Hey, Ray, I've read your manuscript – great work by the way, but this is what I'm thinking of doing, a bit of slashing and limb-lopping, how's that sit with you? A conversation is all I'm saying, Gordon. A dialogue. You owed me that, surely. I might have been able to swallow this one and gone with you, but not like this. Not with this *fait accompli* that you've dumped upon me. So, where does this leave us?

Don't get me wrong, Gordon, what you've done is outstanding. Your insights are extraordinary. In reading the edit I had the strange feeling of dreaming someone else's dreams: they were like mine but oddly not mine. Two-thirds of the edit is fine, I think, remarkable even. Better than anything that I could ever hope to write with or without your hand up my back. But the other stories, there's five or six of them; what you've done to them turns my guts. You have always had such a great surgical nose for literary gangrene and you've never been shy of hacking off the dead flesh, but the gross butchering of these... Man, it turns my guts. How could you? Look at what I gave you and look at your amputations. The limbless things you hacked up bear no resemblance to the lively stories that I gave you to improve. They're barely surviving on life support. They need to be grafted and restored to health. That is my preference. If you can't do that then pull the plug on them. They can't come out like mangled freaks. I won't allow that. Fix them or kill them, I don't care which. But I guess without those stories there is not enough for a book. So fix them or no book.

Look, Gordon, I don't mean to sound ungrateful. Everything that I am and everything that I have now is due to no-one but you, and to the faith you have shown in me for more than a decade. The debt I owe you is beyond recompense. You have looked deeper and further into me than I have ever dared to do. And you have always made my stories more perfect because of this. Like what you did with the book title ... yes, that nice piece of poetic repetition, why I can only dream that I had created that. Sometimes I wonder why you bothered with me at all because your vision of the stories and themes and characters was so much clearer than mine. I felt so shallow compared to you. And mostly you were right. I don't want to lose your love or respect over this, Gordon, but my overwhelming debt to you is clouding my judgement. I want so desperately to believe you are right on this, in all of this, but there is a fragile new part of me that is not so sure. Tess asked me recently if you were my ideal reader. Jesus! What blasphemy! How could I doubt you? You have supported and championed me and my writing from the beginning. You have been the one and only stable point in my turbulent world of booze, teaching, adultery and kids. I am behind you one hundred percent. I want this book so much. I need this book. But I'm scared of this book too.

I'll let you in on where I'm coming from on this. You see, it's these new stories, the longer ones, that I can't let go of because they, well, how do I say this without sounding trite? These stories, well, they saved me. I don't mean this lightly. They saved me from driving too fast around a mountain bend or crashing at night on the expressway. They saved me from shooting myself in the bathroom, or gassing myself in the garage, or drowning in a cocktail of booze and pills. These stories, like the others, may have their bleak moments, but there is a ray of hope in them too. Take for instance ... yes, that one. I read it, your edit, and I don't see the essence of what I wrote in it. I mean, I gave you 30-odd pages and you cherry-pick from the first half of the story and toss away the second half! Is that what you think I meant? Because your edit makes no sense to me at all. I just see a hack job, a Civil War medical tent with bloody limbs tossed into the corner and you gritting your teeth as you rip away at another leg with that bloody hacksaw. And I see that it is me on the table, and they are my fucking limbs that you are sawing off and I can't do a fucking thing about it. Gordon, do you see this? Does it trouble you to make me feel this way?

No? ... No. Really? ... But it's not you whose name will be on the jacket cover. Perhaps it should read 'stories by Raymond Carver, edited by Gordon Lish'. Don't tell me you haven't thought of it.

It's what people will say that scares me most. Did you write this? Yes, but... They are my babies. They were all born wonderful in my eyes but now they've come out all wrong. Look, I've got friends who have read all these stories, including the ones you have been most severe with. And they love them as they are, untouched, as I wrote them. What am I supposed to say to them when they see these amputations appear? How am I to hold these hacks truly as my own?

I can't be the fall guy on this one. I am not your piece of clay to mold, and these stories are too much of my own sweat and piss and blood and shit and semen for me to let them go. Get me out of this book, Gordon. I'll do anything. I'll post back the advance. I'll get on my knees for you. I'll loose a turd on the publisher's desk. Anything. I want the book but this is too much, Gordon, this edit is too much. I want so much to do this book with you, my legs tremble with the need for it, but not like this. No, not like this. You have me bent over the table, my pants around my ankles. Your hands clamp my crossed arms on my lower back. The fleshy helmet of your hard cock presses insistently at the asterisk of my ass. And you're … oh God, Gordon. A roaring comes over me. A lamp flares and pops. The room falls away. I don't move.

Sisyphus of the Simpson Desert

There was a time, I'm sure, when this was a punishment, but I've been doing it so long now that I can't recall when that might have been. Nor can I remember what offence I may have committed, or against whom, who the prosecutor was, or who the judge, not even the terms of the sentence. But there must have been a crime. Why else would I be here? Now I am only aware of physical effort. A labour. A gargantuan labour. And I endure it, willingly. This is, I think, the second phase. I don't know if there is a third phase, and if there is, what it will entail.

Again I am at the base of the sandhill attached to a cart loaded with food and water and equipment that is twice my own body weight. The sun sneaks across my right shoulder. A hot and dry head-wind. No shade.

I begin to climb, pushing hard on poles, kicking toeholds in the sand. The heavy cart resists. I climb a knife-edge so sharp I could be cleaved in two. Cells exert maximum power. Blood gushes, high pressure. Arteries throb. Veins bulge. Breath shallow, rapid. Muscles tendons fascia strain. Lean forward. Press forward. Gasp. Grind.

Stop. Strain to hold position. Halfway, maybe. Sweat cascades my brow. Eyes sting. Mouth dry and pasty. I take a swig of water. Mouth dry and pasty. Lungs heave. I feel like a drag car at the starting grid, engine thrashing and wheels spinning and rubber burning, but when the lights go green and the handbrake drops the engine blows.

I rock forward and back with shoulders and hips, forward and back, forward and back again, and with an explosion of breath I thrust and haul and slog and step. I'm moving up, and tug and step, heave and step, slowly up keep going, pull and step, argh! one more step, one more step … until I reach the crest and double over, fall to my knees, gasping for air, blood thumping at my temples.

There is no euphoria at reaching the summit, only a brief respite before the burden rolls forward and accelerates down the slope with me still attached, pushing me, threatening to overrun me and impale me on the javelins of spinifex. After all the effort of ascent, it seems almost natural to be down at the base again where there is nowhere else to go but up. There is only up.

If I knew the terms of my sentence, such as that there were a finite number of repetitions of this sapping toil up (and down) these monstrous sandhills, then that would truly be a punishment. I would be counting them down, scratching their mark along the length of my arms and legs and chest and face. At the beginning I would despair at how hard and how unfair was the labour, and how far away my release. And as the end crept closer, so near as to almost touch me, then the remaining sandhills would grow in size and difficulty in direct proportion with the desire for release.

I remember nothing about my sentence, and I am grateful for that. If there is no prospect of release, no limit to the number of times I climb these sandhills, then the notion of punishment is redundant.

So, you want to know: How many I have climbed? How many do I have to go? Or stated another way: Is there an end to all of this? And: Will I make it?

I am climbing this one.

aka

If names are not correct, language will not be in accordance with the truth of things.
   Confucius

1.

*M*y full name is Jeffery James JAMESON.[1] *I was born at P—— on 17 A—— 1965. My parents' names are Beverley Anne JAMESON and Martin Clifford JAMESON. My mother's maiden surname is JAMES. I have one older brother, Shaun Martin JAMESON, whose date of birth is 27 J—— 1964.*[2]

The fact of my birth is incontestable. Dr Cox and Sister Sullivan recorded the details and Mr JL Rath of Melbourne, clerk, meticulously typed them onto the scheduled form, flicking the return bar of his typewriter after every end-line comma or period.

---

1. The names and details of the author and his kin have been altered to protect them from the shame of identity theft.
2. The italicised text throughout this section of the document is from the signed statement of the author taken as evidence in August 1999 by Federal Agent Cook.

Name.
Sex.
Father.
Occupation.
Married.
Previous issue (living and deceased).
Mother.

The completed form was proof: I have been registered, therefore I exist.

I have a copy of that form, printed on baby-boy blue paper in 1973. The full birth certificate of Jeffery James Jameson was required at that time for my first identity papers: an Australian passport for a family holiday. The blue form would emerge over the years to prove that I was I, and no other. It secured for me a drivers licence eleven years later, and another passport seven years after that.

In January 1996 I flew to South America on Australian passport K0469662 issued in my birth name and returned twelve months later. After clearing customs I called my mother, let her know I had returned safely and would see her the next day. There was relief in her voice, but also a hint of uncertainty: 'ASIC called a couple of weeks ago. They want to speak with you.'

ASIC. The Australian Securities and Investments Commission is Australia's independent regulator of the corporate and financial sectors. Among its many roles is the power to investigate and prosecute white-collar crime such as company fraud, bankruptcy and insider trading.

For several years prior to going to South America I had worked as an analyst/programmer for a share registry software company that managed the dividends and floats of Australia's public companies. And I personally maintained the software of one of the nation's largest trust funds, Colonial Mutual (whose first company president, Sir Redmond Barry, sentenced Ned Kelly to be hung).

Was my mother worried? Wondering if I had siphoned off share dividends? Allocated myself bonus shares in the Commonwealth Bank float? Or given a trader inside information? After all, how well do we really know our children and siblings? What needs drive them? What shameful secrets do they hide? A friend of mine, a talented chemist, had recently been busted and sent to prison for five years for running a meth lab from his home in the Dandenongs. A close friend. I was the quiet type. Maybe I wasn't so clean. How could she be sure?

The next day we hugged for the first time in a year and she joked: 'Ah! Here's my wandering son. What's his name?'

She handed me the message: *Call Glen Cook, ASIC.* As I dialled the number she asked me something about meditation or chakras, I'm not sure which, but before I could clarify he answered. He was direct: 'How did you get back into the country without me hearing about it?'

I have never given permission for another person to use my name.

It's not like I snuck in under an assumed name, or emerged from a shipping container at the Melbourne dockyards, paying the last instalment of cash to the ship's captain and the welcoming stevedore.

I came through immigration with my Australian passport in my own name at Tullamarine airport. I waited in the red queue. My bags were searched, and two film canisters containing green leaf fragments were pulled from the bottom of my pack. Idiot, I berated myself, why didn't I throw them out? The customs officer straightened his cap and looked right at me. He opened the suspicious containers. He licked his fingertip, inserted it, smelt and tasted it. He spat.

'What is this?'

'Ah, that one is oregano, the other is basil.' The canisters were confiscated. The incident recorded.

I took a few minutes to repack. 'Welcome home,' the customs officer finally said, returning my passport, 'Mr Jameson.' I emerged through the one-way sliding doors without anyone putting a hand on my shoulder.

The morning following the phone call I met Mr Cook (actually, Federal Agent Cook) in the lobby of a Collins Street high-rise. We shook hands. I looked at his loose grey suit. He looked over my Doc Martens, Levi jeans and buzz-cut. We sat in a lobby sofa. An informal chat, I surmised, not requiring the intimidation of an office. He leant towards me: 'How do you know Charles K———?'

I do not recall having ever met any person or persons by the names of Charles K[3] or Charles Edward GENTRY.

'About 5 feet 10, Caucasian, Egyptian parents, mid-thirties ...' He described him as a cop in a cheap detective novel would. Showed me a passport-sized photo. A broader face, stockier build. If we stood in a police line-up next to each other no-one would ever think we were related.

'Have you ever met him?'

'Charles K?'

'Yes.'

Chucky? A great guy! We met in a grungy Footscray pub ... no ... no ... he wouldn't be seen dead there ... we met in a rooftop bar at the top of Collins Street, you know, the one with the full-length windows in the bathroom overlooking the city lights. I pulled a note from the fold of green bills he handed me and we did some lines of coke. Before we parted I raised a toast to him: *¡Feliz cumpleaños!* Literally, Happy Nameday!

'I ask you this,' Agent Cook said, interrupting my daydream, 'because Mr K is involved in an investigation of mine.'

---

3. For simplicity and readability, from this point Charles K——— will be referred to as Charles K.

'But what's that ...' I looked at him and gulped, '... what's that got to do with me?' I wished that I was still trekking in Patagonia. I wished that I was anywhere but here.

'Among the evidence that was found in K's possession,' Agent Cook continued, 'was ID for a number of aliases, about a dozen of them, and all but two lead nowhere. All but two,' he repeated, continuing to eyeball me. 'Those two both emanate from your name.'

'From me!' I said, incredulous. 'How?'

'That's what I want to know. Your name was legally changed twice ...'

'What?'

'... twice in the past two years. K is in possession of ID relating to both of the aliases Cinclair and Gentry. Tracing those names leads to the "legal" change of your name, to you, the only real person in our search. So: how did he obtain the ID to change your name?'

I have never changed my name through the Victorian Registry of Births, Deaths and Marriages.

I was too stunned to speak.

Agent Cook related the facts. On 16 March 1995, a change of name was registered and approved for a Jeffery James Jameson of 4/10 Larnoo Avenue, West Brunswick to be known henceforth as Carlton James Cinclair, the reason being that he was 'joining the army' and 'the name would be more adequate'. Then on 5 August 1996 in Sunnybank Hills, Queensland, a change of name was registered for a Jeffery James Jameson (with the same parents' details and birth date as stated in the previous change of name request) of 50 Darebin Road, Thornbury, to be known as Charles Edward James Gentry. The 'previous name change' box was marked 'no'. The oversight was noticed and noted. The name Jeffery James Jameson no longer existed so it could not be altered again. Perhaps the applicant was contacted and provided new documentation, perhaps not. At any rate, two days later a name change certificate was issued for the name change from Carlton James Cinclair to Charles Edward James Gentry.

Certain government departments, such as Immigration & Citizenship, are informed of name changes so they can scour their databases for illegal activities by the applicant: fraud, bankruptcy, sex offences, on bail or parole, detainee, prisoner. Agent Cook at ASIC began investigating the name changes in November 1996.

'I haven't lived at either of those addresses,' I said. 'Not even in the northern suburbs.' And in August 1996 I was on a boat cruising around the Galapagos Islands.

The agent inferred that I might have sold my identity to K, that I received some kind of benefit, possibly of the order that would allow one year of overseas travel.

'No,' I flatly denied.

'I will need a statement from you. Not right now, but soon.' He handed me a copy of the two name change applications and stood.

'How can I change it back?' I asked, but when I looked up from the forms in my hand he had gone.

I have never given permission for any other person to change my name through the Victorian Registry of Births, Deaths and Marriages.

What personal identification do you need to change your name? A birth certificate, an ID card (Medicare, student, debit or credit card), and an authorised witness (such as a bank manager or doctor—someone you may never have met before and would never meet again) to sign the form, confirming that you are who you claim to be, or at the very least, possess the necessary identification to make that claim. In the not too distant future, identity checks would become more stringent, adding a signed photo ID (passport or drivers licence), and proof of address (phone or utilities bill, or lease agreement) to the mandatory requirements. But in 1996, with a birth certificate and a student ID card, you could be anyone. How difficult were such documents to obtain? As I sat in the lobby, I tried to recall the few times in recent years that I had used my full birth certificate. And then I remembered receiving a replacement Medicare card last year. When was that? March? The old card had not expired and was still in my wallet, and despite Medicare's claim, I had not ordered the replacement card, which had a different number from the old one. At the time I thought it was odd, but not odd enough to report. Was this relevant or mere coincidence?

I walked out of the high-rise and turned right without thinking. I felt light-headed, a bit shaky, and a cool sweat covered me. I reached for a seat at a street-side café and sat lightly. I looked down at my hands on the table and for a moment I saw right through them. When I felt more solid I got up and walked on, absent-minded. Before I realised where I was going I stood at the entrance to the Victorian Registry of Births, Deaths and Marriages. I fronted up to the glass-windowed counter.

'Name, please.'

I summed up the situation: my name, that it had been changed by someone else, twice, without my prior knowledge or consent, and was now such-and-such, and that I wanted it changed back.

'That is not possible.'

'But why not? It's my name.'

'So you say.' The clerk informed me that they process around 250 name changes a week, that the application form is a legal document and name change applications are rigorously checked. 'Once approved and registered, it cannot be nullified,' he concluded.

'So ... there is nothing...'

'If what you claim is true, that a certain person has made a false declaration, then that person can be charged with *wilful and corrupt perjury* and is liable to the penalties of perjury as stated in the Crimes Act 1958 section 314.'

'Meaning...'

'A maximum of fifteen years. And the fraudulent actions would, of course, be annulled; that is, the name changes would be wiped.'

The only name that I have ever used has been Jeffery James JAMESON.

I have used a pseudonym at times for things I have written, but that was not done to deceive. Most people know me by a nickname and would have to guess what my real name is. I am 'Jay-Jay' obviously, and I was 'Triple-J' long before FM radio came about.

And then there was a barista at a sandwich place on St Kilda Road that for years called me Andrew, but I'm certain I never introduced myself to him, that he just called me Andrew one day, like 'How ya going, Andrew?' in a friendly way while he made my café latte and small talked about footy or the weather and I wasn't sure that I heard him right and since I thought he might have confused me with someone else I didn't bother to correct him, and then the next time I saw him he asked politely how I—well, actually, how Andrew—was, and two years later I still hadn't objected or corrected him. He may as well have called me 'mate' because that's the way I took it.

Once I went there with a colleague named Andrew. The barista smiled and asked 'The usual, Andrew?' while looking at me. I nodded. Andrew said 'Yes' with a puzzled look on his face. While the coffee machine squealed Andrew turned to me, 'I've never been here before. How does he know my name and what I drink?' Everyone drank lattes then; we hadn't evolved to flat whites or doppio ristrettos. I shrugged and laughed, then confessed in a low voice after collecting our coffees, 'He was talking to me. It's a private joke of sorts between us, although I'm not sure if the joke is on me or on him. He's called me Andrew for almost two years. I don't have the heart to tell him that he's confused me with someone else.' And to myself I muttered, 'Just in case he hasn't.'

I have only ever applied for an Australian passport in my name of Jeffery James JAMESON.

I checked the forms Agent Cook had given me. Clearly they had been filled in by the same person; the handwriting was identical.

The letter R was capitalised wherever it was used. The camber of the text was skewed, like a backslash, a likely indication of the writer being left-handed. The signature was not written with a flourish—rather it was printed in the same round-lettered script that was used to fill in the entire application. It was as if a warped mirror, something from the Fun House at Luna Park, had been held to my sharp-pointed and angled-right script. If Agent Cook had asked me for a handwriting sample then it would have been immediately obvious that I had not completed or signed the documents, but then he may have already obtained samples of my handwriting and signature from the bank, or from Immigration.

My life was in bureaucratic limbo. According to the Victorian Registry of Births, Deaths and Marriages, Jeffery James Jameson no longer existed—he was now Charles Edward James Gentry, and all of his identity documents should be in the new name. But I was still living as Jeffery James Jameson, with bank account, drivers' licence, passport, tax file number, vehicle registration, and other identification, all stating that I was he. My assets and bank account had not been frozen or redirected to Charles Edward James Gentry.

I recalled a scene in *Catch-22* (New York, 1961) where Doc Daneeka witnesses his own death by administration. Doc feared death and flying equally, but he had to log a minimum amount of flight time to collect a bonus. So he did a deal with one of the pilots who put him on his passenger manifest, thereby getting his hours without having to leave the ground. Doc was proud of his scam, laughing while he watched his pilot do acrobatic sweeps of the beach. But when that plane dived towards the cliff and the sergeant standing next to him confirmed that Doc was on the manifest and prayed for him to bail out, Doc whimpered 'I'm right here', but how could he be here when the manifest said he was up there and the manifest was never wrong. When the plane crashed into the cliff without the mushrooming of any parachutes, the sergeant bowed his head and said 'Poor Doc' because Doc was now legally dead even though he still stood there whimpering 'I'm right here' long after the sergeant walked away.

'I'm right here,' I echoed after a long silence and no-one took any notice.

I feared for my future. Would I be able to leave the country again? Obtain another passport when the current one expired? Get married? Could any illegal deeds performed in the name of Charles Edward James Gentry and Carlton James Cinclair be linked or attributed to me?

I have only ever travelled overseas in my name Jeffery James JAMESON. I have never travelled into or out of Australia or any other country in the name of Carmello Jiovanni CANTICA.

It is said that everyone has a double somewhere. What if I met mine during one wild night of partying and we did a deal to give him a new identity? He could be the opposite of me, anything he wanted.

Since early 1995, perhaps earlier, there was at least one other version of me, my *hrönir*, walking around Melbourne and doing things in my name. And on 16 March 1995, with the aid of the unique details on the baby-boy blue form, one of them cut me out and gave itself a new identity. And a year later, another mutation occurred. There was now me, Jeffery James Jameson, and at least two or three others: a pseudo-Jeffery James Jameson, Carlton Cinclair, and Charles Gentry.

Whenever I thought about them I was stumped by the same questions about my identity theft and nameless-ness. What was their motivation? What did they stand to gain? (Or conversely, what did they risk losing if they did not obtain a new identity?) And most importantly: Would I ever get my birth name back? I could speculate, but I only got wound up in knots of pulp fiction.

A couple of years passed without any contact from Agent Cook or correspondence from the authorities, and for my part, I did not pursue the matter. With a growing combination of relief and apathy, I stopped worrying and started to forget about Charles K and Charles Gentry. They were like a dark freckle on my skin that looked like it could lead to skin cancer, that I should get checked or cut out, but after years it hadn't changed size so I thought it must be benign, and if it wasn't then I really didn't want to know, and stopped thinking about it. Like that.

Neither Charles K nor Charles Gentry objected to me getting married in December 1997, or stopped me from leaving the country the following year. They did not bid against me at auction, or refuse to grant me a new passport when the old one expired. I vote. I pay tax. And I do it all as Jeffery James Jameson. No authority, other than the Registry of Births, Deaths and Marriages, deems me a non-person.

And then in August 1999 Agent Cook contacted me, producing a statement that I read and signed. And then? Nothing. More than a decade passed. They never let me know the outcome.

A recent web search brought up this May 2000 media release from ASIC:

> Former Victorian businessman Charles K was today sentenced to a 12 month suspended jail sentence after pleading guilty to six ASIC charges.
>
> Mr K was charged with three counts of obtaining property by deception, two counts of using a passport of another to travel out of and into Australia, and one count of failing to appear on bail.
>
> Mr K was to stand trial on the first three counts of obtaining property by deception but failed to appear. He travelled out of Australia from Darwin on 1 August 1997 two days before the scheduled trial on a passport in the name of Carmello Jiovanni Cantica. He returned to Australia eight months later on a passport in the name of Charles Lucas Turlington.

Mr K was extradited from Queensland by the Australian Federal Police after serving a jail term for fraud-related offences.

There was no mention of him being charged with wilful and corrupt perjury, or of him possessing ID relating to numerous other aliases. No mention at all of Charles Edward James Gentry or Carlton James Cinclair or Jeffery James Jameson.

It wasn't over. He had not been punished. He was still me. And who were the other people mentioned?

I have never used the names Carlton James CINCLAIR, Charles Edward James GENTRY, Carmello Jiovanni CANTICA, Charles CARRERAS nor Charles Christian DENEUVE.

Charles Gentry became Carmello Jiovanni Cantica in 1997, applied for and received an Australian passport then skipped the country before Charles K's trial in August. He returned to Australia as Charles Lucas Turlington in March 1998. A few months later, Cantica became Charles Carreras. And one year later, in 1999, shortly before Charles K was arrested in Queensland, Carreras became Charles Christian Deneuve. What a cluster-fuck! Five iterations of the name, and three of them occurring after Charles K was pending trial. Why wasn't a freeze or alert placed on the name so it couldn't be changed again?

But it doesn't end there. Charles K continues not only to use, but to live by, the name Charles Gentry. Under that guise he has become a minor celebrity and media personality, producing several reality-TV shows, and occasionally gracing the gossip columns of Sydney tabloids, for better or for worse.

Meanwhile, I continue to live as Jeffery James Jameson, but without ownership of the name. If I wanted, for any reason, to legally change my name in the future to something like, Michael James Giacometti, for example, then the application would be denied.

'Having a birth certificate in the original name is not enough,' the clerk at the Registry would say. 'You require a full name change certificate in the current legal name: Charles Christian Deneuve.'

'Can I request such a certificate?'

'Do you have the necessary forms of photo and other ID in the said name?'

'No, I don't.'

'Then no. Only the legal owner of the name can request a copy of the full name change certificate. You are not that person.' No. I would need to commit a fraud in order to correct a fraud.

And there it stands—a confusion of names for future family genealogists to unravel into a branch and biographical sketch on the family tree.

When I die there will be no neat administrative closure at the Registry. The clerk will find no matching birth record with which to bracket the death of Jeffery James Jameson, and likewise, Charles Christian Deneuve will live on after my death, only to be presumed dead when he reaches the grand age of 100 years.

2.

In February 2012, after fifteen years of inaction and at the prompting of the author, the recently rebranded Births Deaths Marriages Victoria launched an official investigation into this matter. The results are pending.

Eildon, August 2012

3.

He called.

Calls himself Charles Duprix now, but it was him, unmistakably him—Charles K.

In almost twenty years, I never once tried to contact him. Didn't know how. Didn't want to. I would Google his name and aliases now and then to see what they were up to. There wasn't much to find. For a self-proclaimed international recording artist and reality-TV producer he was shy of internet exposure. Then yesterday, I found him on a social networking site.

I posed as a freelance journalist writing an article about people who have changed their name, the reasons why, and the impact that the name change has had on their life, work and wellbeing. I offered the prospect of a national readership. I hoped for, but did not expect, a reply.

I put Elvis Presley's *Memphis* album (1969) in the CD player. A few songs in, the twirling guitar and insistent drum introduced 'Suspicious Minds' and Elvis crooned the opening line … *We're caught in a trap* … as the phone rang. A blocked number; untraceable. All my senses focused on the ringing. I choked on the greeting, 'Hell—'

'Jeffery? Before I say anything, I want to know who you are, who you work for, and how you got on to me.' By the time the song faded and the funereal peals of the piano introduced the next track, I had assuaged him enough for us to proceed with the interview (or the charade of one).

Charles K was born in Alexandria, Egypt in August 1972 and moved to Australia three years later. He is legally known as Charles K, but has used the stage names Charles Gentry and Charles Duprix, and no other. Duprix is his mother's maiden name.

'Why did you change your stage name mid-career? Surely that is a risky move for a media personality.'

He was a Bollywood movie star, had a residency singing in Las Vegas, and had been offered movie and record deals. 'Everyone loved me,' he said. Except the gossip press, who delighted in publishing trashy stories about him, all lies, he claimed. But the movie and record deals fell through. The name 'Charles Gentry' got so it stank. His producers suggested a fresh identity.

It was surreal to be having a conversation with the man who, allegedly, took my name. K's voice was the aural equivalent of Dorian Gray's portrait. I would not have this opportunity again. I wanted him to own up to what he had done to me. And I wanted to know why.

'I want to read you a list of names,' I said. 'Have you ever heard (or used, I almost said) any of these: Carlton James Cinclair, Charles Carreras, Charles Christian Deneuve, Charles Turlington?' I read them one at a time. To each he replied categorically 'No.' 'Carmello Jiovanni Cantica?' I stumbled over the pronunciation in an English way: CAN-ti-ca. 'Can-TEE-ca,' he corrected me, putting the emphasis on the correct syllable, 'no.'

He could not hear my raised eyebrows. I decided on a more direct line. 'Charles, I want to read you an ASIC press release...'

'ASIC?'

'Yes, ASIC.'

'Where did you get that?' he said sharply. 'What's ASIC got to do with this?'

'From their website. An ASIC press release dated...' I read the document in full. 'So, do you still deny knowing the name Carmello Cantica?'

'That was so long ago, what has it got to do with ...' He paused. 'Okay, yes, I did use a passport in that name, but it was given to me by a friend. He let me put my photo on his passport application.'

'And what was his name?'

'Cantica. Carmello Cantica.'

'And where is he now, your friend?'

'He has gone back to Italy.'

'So you left Australia on a passport in the name of Carmello Jiovanni Cantica a couple of days before your trial for obtaining property by deception was to commence.'

'Yes, but I was looking at ten years jail for something I never did. Have you seen that Harrison Ford movie, *The Fugitive* (1993), where he has to prove his innocence by going on the run? Well, that's what I was doing.'

At 26 years of age, Charles K was a director in a company that joined with a Melbourne media mogul to purchase and refurbish a Melbourne nightclub. The refurbishment ran overtime and millions over budget. They were forced to sell up at an incredible loss. Having briefly lived the high-life, Charles K was bankrupt.

He got a job working for a cousin from the United States, investing in speculative (and with the near 20 per cent interest rates at the time, potentially lucrative) strata title office developments. The business bubbled and burst. His cousin fled to America leaving Charles K as the fall guy. 'I was not a director or a partner in the business. I was an employee. But they wanted to pin everything on me.'

'So, yes, I used the Cantica passport to get out of Australia to avoid an eight-week trial and ten years in jail, and I used the Turlington passport to return to Australia without being caught. It has been alleged that I used other names, but there is no truth to it. And that ASIC case, all the charges were dropped. Nothing came of it.' But that is not entirely true. The charges weren't dropped. Charles K pleaded guilty to all 6 counts, and received 12 months suspended sentence.

'My life is transparent,' he said. 'I am answering everything you ask.' He was forthcoming with information, much of which I had no knowledge of, but I couldn't say that he had been open and honest. No. His past as presented was a dense fog.

'I don't care what you do with this stuff, but slander or defame me and my lawyers will be all over you. I've got a $50 million lawsuit against a broadcast company, the largest suit in Australia, that's been going since 2011.'

A bleat of horns introduced the final Elvis song from his celebrated comeback TV special in 1968. Those horns and the opening line, *There must be lights burning brighter, somewhere...* are forever associated with the vision of a young man in a white suit standing alone in the spotlight in front of a large red neon sign emblazoned with his name, a young man trying with every note of his fine voice to re-establish his former pre-eminence, and now they are inextricably linked to Charles Duprix.

We spoke for an hour.

We hung up on good terms, like we were cousins who had reconnected after many years apart. I felt less of a victim, and that he was equally as much a victim of circumstance as I. I wanted to believe that he told the truth, but there were some inconsistencies in his testimony, and the nagging doubt kept tapping at my temple: Is he scamming me? What are his words worth? What is he getting out of confessing to me?

He categorically denied any knowledge of, or participation in, any unlawful activity relating to changing the name of Jeffery James Jameson, despite the coincidence that two of the aliases that he used were the same as those that my name had been changed to: Gentry and Cantica. Despite his protestation, how could I be sure? I had no proof that he had actually done anything. It was his word against no other.

I watched *The Fugitive* (1993), the movie that K referred to. I watched *The Usual Suspects* (1995) with Kevin Spacey as Roger 'Verbal' Kint, who, under interrogation, weaves a complex story about Keyser Söze that in the end is revealed as something else, a labyrinth of lies and inventions. I watched these movies for clues, and for inspiration. It was irrational. I filled notebooks with intrigues.

I needed more information, but from where?

I grabbed the ASIC press release. The obtaining property by deception charges related to offences that occurred in 1990. By his own reckoning, Charles K would have been 18 years old. But the Melbourne nightclub fiasco happened prior to this, and Charles K stated that he was 26 years old at that time.

This timeline anomaly was quickly cleared up in the media mogul's memoir (Rigby, 1999). It was 1988. Charles K was hired to manage the nightclub being renovated. He had his office fitted out with a marble en-suite and gold taps. He demanded a red Ferrari. There was messy public falling out, reported in the *Truth*. Charles K was sacked. He sued for breach of contract, and settled out of court for $50,000 in early 1989. But why would Charles K perjure himself about his age? What was he hiding?

In past readings of the ASIC press release, I had always been stumped by the lack of detail and penalty regarding the name changes. Was it raised in that court? And if not, why not? If I were to find any answers, then they would be in the trial transcripts.

The Queen v Charles K (Melbourne, 2000) revealed another Charles K. Born in Egypt on 19 August 1962 (liar—not 1972), he moved with his family to Australia in 1965. He had some success as a pre-teen singer. He completed a Diploma of Business and Marketing at RMIT and worked in clubs and hotels. He achieved heady business success at a young age but then had difficulty coping with financial ruin. He became depressed, and his unclear thinking led him to flee the country prior to trial in August 1997. His depression was in part due to the inordinate length of time between the offences occurring (1990), the charges being laid (October 1994) and the trial date (August 1997). Consequently, there was a 10-year gap between the date of the initial offences, and them coming to trial. For that decade, Charles K's business life was essentially on hold. On the phone Charles K could have mentioned this as a reason for absconding, but he didn't; he said he left to avoid a long trial and a lengthy jail sentence *and* to prove his innocence. Liar.

With regard to the obtaining property by deception charges, the judge stated that many people in the company were involved in the fraud, that they were not Charles K's sole or direct fault, and the judge was, to a degree, satisfied that Charles K had subsequently done his utmost to make full financial restitution for the offences.

And the passport offences, the use of passports in the name of Cantica and Turlington, were mentioned but not how they were obtained. There was no mention of Gentry or any other aliases other than that upon his return to Australia in March 1998 he lived in Queensland using the false ID of Carmello Jiovanni Cantica.

I had it wrong all along. I had been chasing a formless shadow for too long. The ASIC trial in Melbourne had nothing to do with my name being changed. If it had been dealt with at all, it was in Queensland.

4.

The Queen v. Charles Edward Gentry, alias Charles K (Brisbane, 1999) was the final lead. Charles K pleaded guilty to 31 fraud-related offences including forgery, uttering and misappropriation (with several of these crimes being of the more serious 'aggravated' nature), in what the judge described as 'a sophisticated course of dishonesty ... which resulted in a successful series of frauds.' He received three years, suspended after six months. After serving the six months, he was sent to Victoria and retained in custody pending his ASIC trial.

On 15 October 1996, Charles K pulled into a shopping complex on the Gold Coast. Maybe he didn't indicate properly, or he parked his sports car in a handicapped space. Maybe the police didn't like the look of him, or maybe they felt like being arseholes. 'Can I see your drivers' licence,' one ordered. 'Thank you, Mr...' the officer hesitated with the pronunciation. 'Gentry,' said Charles K. The officer looked at the photo on the licence and back at the name. 'Please step out of the car, Mr Gentry,' the officer said, opening the door, 'or is it Mr Contorro?'

The car was searched. The police found five Queensland drivers' licences all containing the same image of Charles K, and all with different names. They were quality forgeries, having been produced with authentic government-issue card and laminate.

A search of his premises unearthed much more. Another four Queensland drivers licences with the same image of Charles K and new names, SIM cards with handwritten names of false identities on them, five blank Victorian birth certificates with the same serial number, and a document containing a list of the many aliases used by Charles K including their date and place of birth. And most importantly (to me, anyway), there were three Victorian birth certificates, two of them being in the name Charles Edward Gentry but with different date of birth, parents and other details. One contained Charles K's real details, the other had my birth-date, my parents. This is what I had been searching for.

I was never shown a full list of the aliases used by Charles K, and though the trial transcript did not mention Jeffery James Jameson at all, I was now certain that Charles K was in possession of my name.

Using the forged ID of Charles Jacob Charra (for whom he had a Victorian birth certificate, Queensland drivers licence, National Australia Bank account statement), and also two other identities, Vincenzo and Contorro, Charles K obtained loans from banks, and lines of credit from department stores, to purchase electronics and whitegoods for resale. When nabbed through nothing but luck by police, the scam had been running for two weeks, and had secured over $25,000 from at least four establishments without raising suspicion. He was poised to defraud much more, up to $100,000.

Some mysteries in the patchy timeline were resolved. In March 1995, my name was changed by an unidentified person to Carlton James Cinclair. In August 1996, that name was changed in Queensland to Charles Edward James Gentry. On 15 October 1996, Charles K was arrested for possessing false identification. During the fraud investigation in November, ASIC became involved. I returned from a year in South America in December 1996. The ASIC offences were set to be tried on 3 August 1997; the Queensland fraud trial was set for 2 September 1997. The maximum penalty for the ASIC charges was 10 years; for the Queensland frauds, 14 years. Bail conditions for the Queensland trial were removed on 25 July 1997. One week later, Charles K skipped the country and both trials using a false identity. He returned using another false identity in March 1998. He was not apprehended until 17 July 1999, over 16 months after returning to Australia and living under an assumed name. The Australian Federal Police obtained a statement from me in August 1999, but by that time, the trial of Charles K in Queensland had already commenced.

At his Queensland trial, Charles K had one more card to play. 'Your Honour, there are extenuating circumstances for my client's activities,' his counsel said. In 1992, Charles K worked with a mate, Tony Franzone, a gambling addict and would-be gangster. Franzone had run up huge debts with underworld loan sharks and was unable to pay. He asked his friend, 'Mate, I'm in deep shit here. I need 10 grand tomorrow or they'll kill my kid.' Charles K refused. Within days, Franzone was executed gangland-style in front of his wife and child outside their Mt Waverley home.

Four years later, in mid-1996, a family friend of Charles K, Mr Z, approached him for money and help to repay a debt. 'I'm in trouble, they gonna kill me, they gonna cut up my girl.' Mr Z had a scam worked out to get loans and credit using fake ID. 'Easy. No risk. I got an inside in the Transport Department. The papers are good. I get you the ID, you get me money. Simple. What names do you want to be?'

Under duress, Charles K assented, justifying that if it saved his friend then it didn't matter that the scam was illegal. And so Charles K became the cat's paw of Mr Z.

With this revelation, police began investigating Mr Z. A sting operation involving a forged bank cheque and a truckload of electronics from Harvey Norman driven by an undercover cop brought Mr Z down. His premises were searched. Document forging equipment and forged ID documents including birth certificates from Queensland and Victoria were seized. The authorities seemed satisfied that Mr Z was the prime mover of the fraud.

So who is guilty in all this?

Charles K, by his own testimony, is guilty of many accounts of fraud, is guilty of being in possession of ID that came from the illegal changing of my name, is guilty of absconding from the country before two court cases and returned not to face the charges but to stay on the run, and has a history of knowingly breaking the law as if the end justifies itself.

The court system is guilty of mental and emotional abuse of the accused; even those who, like Charles K, plead guilty from the start and wish to make full financial restitution, but are instead left in limbo as their case gets scheduled and adjourned and re-scheduled months and years beyond the offence.

Given this revealed history, Charles K was much more of a victim than I was. I did not begrudge his desire to reinvent himself by losing 10 years and taking a new name, Charles Duprix. After all, he had lost that much of his life due to the after-effects of the Melbourne nightclub fiasco. He did some stupid things, made some poor decisions, but he paid for them in many ways.

Somehow this obsessive search had become more about Charles K (or Gentry or Duprix), about proving or disproving the facts of his existence, than it was about finding out or reclaiming the existence of Jeffery James Jameson. And despite his lies and untruths, despite his duplicity and perjury, I empathised with him, I merged with him, and so became less than myself.

I never expected that the trail would become so twisted. Knowing now that Charles K was found guilty of possessing my name in 1999, why hadn't the name changes been annulled? Was there no communication after the trial between the Queensland Courts, the Australian Federal Police and the Victorian Registry of Births, Deaths and Marriages?

I called Births Deaths and Marriages Victoria. I spoke with the woman who launched the investigation into the name changes of Jeffery James Jameson in 2012. She still worked there. Promoted. She checked the records and called me back.

I wasn't sure what to expect.

'I sent you a letter in December 2013,' she said, 'detailing the result of the investigation.'

I didn't receive any letter. I had changed address.

'The fraudulent name changes have been removed and your original birth name has been reinstated.'

I felt relieved ... and a little deflated. Twenty years. Almost twenty-one.

Somewhere someone died and someone was reborn. I put the phone down and walked out the open door. I stopped and stood, arrested by the bright sunshine. I searched the ground about me and there it was, right there. A full, dark shadow. I smiled and the shadow smiled too. The shadow of Jeffery James Jameson.

5.

Today is World Peace Day. Conflict has been curtailed since midnight (or since sunrise, or from sunset, if you go by the Hindu, or Hebrew calendar, respectively). Tonight I will light a candle for the dead and raise a toast to this makeshift cardboard headstone above a mound in the back yard:

R E S T   I N   P E A C E
Charles Christian Deneuve
(16 March 1995—December 2013)
also known as
Carlton James Cinclair
Charles Edward James Gentry
Carmello Jiovanni Cantica
and Charles Carreras.

Alice Springs, 21 September 2016

The Unnameable

Before man all was formless;
shadows roamed: opaque, nameless.

Once man [spirit-men, our ancestors] has named all the
creatures,
the creatures rename ... [untranslatable].

[...]

[When] Koomanjay in white sends cloaking clouds
south, nothing can be seen.

All is Koomanjay:
unseen, unknown, unnamed.

All is Koomanjay.

from the recently unearthed—unpublished and
poorly translated (Ed.)—Tablet of Koomanjay[1]

---

1. Koomanjay is an Aboriginal word literally meaning 'no name'. The spelling
across the Central and Western Desert languages varies; the version used here is
a phonetic composite.

1.

*S*ir, a bony finger tapped in Morse on the back of his hand. *Sir*, harder this time, *We are approaching —— Creek*. *Sir*, tap-tap-tap, tap-tap, tap-taaap-tap. The translator, M, sat up without seeing the torch or the bright light of it shining in his face. Even if his eyes were still closed he would have no trouble in making out the shape of the man standing over him. He smelt the man's minted breath; he could taste the garlic that the mint was sucked to hide; and he relished the superstitious fear that oozed from the man's glands. M sat up. His night visitor departed, his heavy footsteps landing in time with the rhythmic rallentando clack-clack of the train upon the stapled joins of track.

M dressed in darkness, feeling the shape and texture of each garment. He exited the compartment and bounced south along the corridor.

From outside and through the carriage windows, a stationary observer would have seen a man walking determinedly, as if on a treadmill, but failing to advance despite his regular stride. Many carriages would roll past between the observer and the man. If they wanted to, the two men could reach out and shake hands without difficulty. And finally the caboose would pass and they would be left standing there, foolishly thrusting hands deep into trouser pockets, standing there surrounded by lights and cameras before a backdrop of desert scrub in a back-lot warehouse with someone shouting out: Let's run it again, places everyone.

Inside the carriage, M felt like a ball in a pinball machine, bouncing with Newtonian regularity from one wall to the other

---

When someone dies, their name is considered taboo and cannot be spoken. The name is 'rested' so the spirit of the deceased will not linger. For a year or so, people and places that have the same or similar-sounding name as the deceased cannot be referred to by the unspeakable name. Instead, they are called 'Koomanjay'. So, if a lady called Alice died, others named Alice or Elise or Alicia would be called Koomanjay, the town of Alice Springs would be referred to as Koomanjay Springs, and it would be Koomanjay (not Alice) going down the rabbit hole and attending the Mad Hatter's Tea Party.

with the machine's lurching progress, his woollen jacket rasping like sandpaper on the rough walls.

The train slowed to a geriatric pace as it passed through the station. The train never stopped here, never picked up anything or anyone. There was no raised platform to step out onto, just rammed earth and a single flickering light on a low pole.

The guard who woke M stood beside him in the open doorway, his arm extended, barring the exit. He pulled a lever with his other hand and a rubber object fell from below the door into the night. With a whoosh and crackle of expanding rubber, the slide inflated. The guard placed a hand on M's nearest shoulder and gave a firm push downwards. M sat. What time is it, asked M. We are a little early, replied the guard after consulting his watch, It is just after 4.

The guard placed M's leather satchel into his lap and like a caring father or over-attentive uncle, pushed him down the slide. As his feet touched earth, M compressed his body into a spring, extended his cane out front and stood.

How far to town from here, he called over his shoulder. The answer came readily from the guard's lips. At one step per foot, M computed, three to the yard … that would be 16,500 paces.

Turn a half-step left and follow the road all the way; you can't miss it, the guard added. And, God be with you, he as M turned and tapped forward and was soon lost to the unanimous night.

2.
The local mayor sat on the dented bonnet of his red-dirt spattered Toyota beside the defaced sign that used to say *Welcome to* —— *Creek*, looking south. Out of the gloom, along the dead straight highway, a dark speck grew in size like a tumour. The mayor looked away and squeezed his eyes tight closed and opened them fully. After closing and opening them again, he renewed his southerly gaze. The speck was now clearly a man. Minutes later, the walking metronome, tapping bitumen–gravel bitumen–gravel and quietly counting … -seven, ninety-eight, ninety-nine, five hundred, came to a halt one yard from the ute. In the sudden silence a siren began

to wail. After a long pause the mayor spat sideways and slid from the bonnet and said, Welcome to the morgue. His practised hand found M's. Their affirmation was soft and brief, their eyes averted.

M had known he was approaching the town limit even without the thousands of paces meticulously counted. At some point, without being able to define the exact moment, he realised that the low hum of the deserted highway had been replaced by the buzz of electric fields, the drone of air-conditioners, and something else, something that even to his rigorous senses was, as yet, undescribable.

Hop in, the mayor said, opening the passenger door, I'll show you around.

M felt his way up into the cab, buckled his seatbelt and placed an elbow on the open window frame. The ute spat gravel as it fishtailed back north. The mayor chirped about the town, but it was mainly stuff to uh-huh and nod your head to, nothing more. M listened as much as courtesy demanded but his olfactories were being over-stimulated by an unfamiliar mix of foetid scents. Over there, the mayor pointed to the south-east as he was driving and talking, Those old camps, no-one lives there anymore. But the stink that still comes from them when the sun and wind come up. Something putrid. The fumigation boys have been there twice and sprayed everything then burnt the lot and sprayed it again, but there ain't nothing that can get rid of the haunting stench of death of that damn Pangkarlangu.

Pangkarlangu? asked M. A devil-devil, the mayor explained. It disguises itself as trees or birds or family and calls and sings people, then kills them and eats them raw. Its breath is foul. Dogs cower, won't go near it. White is invisible to it. It hides in shadows, disappears in darkness.

A car with bleating horn accelerated out of a side street ahead of the mayor's ute then skidded to a halt where an ambulance with siren sounding and red lights flashing blocked a lane of the highway. The mayor eased pressure on the accelerator, slowing enough to see the cause of the accident and nod to the attending policewoman who returned a sequence of hand signals.

A killer killer, said the mayor, tipping his head to the crash scene. Eight of them in there, all drunk. Now all dead. The unlicensed and underage driver was over the limit but he was the most sober of the lot, driving an unroadworthy car without plates. Crashed into a cow for tucker and rolled and the roof crushed them.

They continued driving past scattered houses and side streets towards the commercial strip. The mayor had lobbied hard for the train line to run through town parallel to Main Street, where many houses of retail had been built and sold and sold again and were now mostly boarded up. The line speared towards the town's centre but abruptly banked and climbed a small steep rise without one pick blade of cutting—a double bane of the railway, which for expediency prefers straight and level tracks—to skirt the town to the windward, coming no closer than 250 chains. The boom that the town had banked on with the railway had bust them again. Only the pub and bottle shop, petrol station and grocery store did any trade. Any tourist that happened up the highway rapidly refuelled and restocked then drove on.

The mayor's ute limped through town, past what remained of the post office, where dumped sacks of mail were being picked through by crows who cawed the names of addressees to each other; past facades of faded signs and peeling paint, where through windows broken and boarded and ripped open again could be seen cairns of excrement erected on vacant floors. Imagine standing over the rank pile, trousers around your ankles, thrusting your arse out over the pinnacle, holding on to your friends or family, trusting them to hold you up as your wobbly imbalance threatens to topple you onto the filth, and you pucker and push and they laugh as you add your black pudding or brown pebbles or melted wax to the summit of *croquembouche a la kuna*.

The town is cursed, the mayor finally stated, shaking his head, as the ute approached the brewery. M tipped his head slightly to better hear.

3.

There were still many people living in the town who believed that it was built on an important sacred site—much like the conquistadors erecting Catholic churches upon the ruins and foundations of Incan temples—a site of secret men's business, with brutal punishment necessary for any transgression of law. Much had been written about the site, and too much had been revealed in sessions of the High Court where the case was, after a decade of appeal and counter-appeal, declared to the plaintiffs. As restitution, they could have demanded the complete removal and revegetation of the town, down to the last piece of wire and nail, the final gram of concrete and every plastic tube of stormwater pipe. Instead they asked for compensation. They demanded a brewery be built at the site of the most important ceremony stone – a brewery which would be open at all hours for the exclusive patronage of anthropologically ratified and registered traditional owners. The consumption of beverages would be confined to the sacred premises. No take-away permitted. Not just because of humbug—no, this was sacred nectar: for properly initiated men only.

Some wanted to name the pub after the sacred totem, but a senior man, Koomanjay, now deceased, heard the mourning call of the butcherbird and noticed the invisible tracks of emu-feathered feet outside his humpy. To that old man, the warning was clear.

The Federal Minister for Aboriginal Emancipation, a city-born yellafella in a polyester suit, flew in to officially open the building, pulling a curtain string to reveal a plaque with two forgettable names: his, and that of the establishment, which had already been covered by a strip of tape with the new appellation—Animal Bar. The minister smiled broadly for the camera then turned to step inside and christen the place by throwing down a golden ale with his 'cousins'. The bouncer at the door didn't like his suit or his colour. Show me, he said.

I'm the Aboriginal Minister, the minister said.

The bouncer narrowed his eyes and pointed at the minister's crotch. Show me, he repeated.

The minister stammered, shook his head. Then he unzipped the fly of his trousers and flopped out his uncircumcised cock. He was denied entry.

Years passed, but not much else. As the mayor drove M up the main street, a man entered the bar.

The barmaid asked, You got ID? What him name?

Koomanjay, he said, barely audible.

Koomanjay. She said it loudly, to make the whisperer speak louder. Patrons around the bar turned their heads to look. Koomanjay what?

West.

The tapping of fingers on a keyboard and a final, forceful ENTER I'm sorry but there is no Koomanjay West in the system. There is … Adam, Bartolemeus, Franklin, Kane … and Taylon, Tennant and Theophanus and…

The man covered his ears and squeezed closed his eyes. He stumbled backwards as if being man-handled by bouncers. The barmaid continued to call out a litany of Wests, all dead, an incantation that caused sores to erupt spontaneously on the man's face and the exposed skin of his arms. As his mouth opened in a silent scream he fell through the glass and stumbled between two parked cars onto the street just as the mayor drove by.

Fuck, not again, said the mayor, gripping the steering wheel as the ute rolled over the human speed hump. Fucken Koomanjay, fucken curse, he said, pulling over in front of the newsagency. He did not bother checking the manslaughter.

Well, said the mayor, at least it's quicker and cleaner than being drunk-bashed with fists, with rocks, with sticks or bricks, with anything close to hand.

The mayor's words slapped M. Their sting hid a low keening wail whose pitch and intensity rose and fell in waves. From out of the laneway beside the hotel a procession of white-faced people appeared and crossed the road to the dead West. How did they know already? It was as if the string of his life pulled taut had alerted the family, like a strand being tugged on a spider's web. The wailing was primal and incessant. All the Jangalas and Nangalas, their uncles and aunties, fathers and mothers and children mobbed together, sheltering in the communal howl, all plastered in kaolin-white clay: in their hair; on their faces and arms, their exposed chests and backs, their bare feet; and over their belted jeans. The cleansing smoke of eucalypt drifted from flour drums converted into censers carried by the managers, those that confirm the story for this one. The white ones, invisible to malignant evil, lifted the dead West and the procession of mourning slowly carried him to the sorry camp north-east of town.

The town is cursed, said the mayor, plain and simple. There's mobs dying everyday. No-one can work. The town has turned into a never-ending sorry camp. Everyone in black pants and white shirts from one funeral to the next. The undertaker never stops. (But few could pay, so the undertaker had excavated a communal pit west of town that looked like an open-cut mine, and for twenty bucks per, he dumped the dead in hessian sacks and covered them with a smattering of soil. He was on to his second pit.) The Town & Place Names have gazetted the new name, Koomanjay Creek, the mayor continued, and are now considering dropping the 'Creek' because someone here will know some poor bastard called Craig who must surely die sometime soon. The mayor shook his head. Shit, fucken Koomanjay. Look at this shit, he said, tossing the paper at M. You can't read the fucken paper anymore, all the bloody koomanjay-koomanjay, which they've shortened to kumnji. You need to be a cryptic crossword genius with a degree in nomenclature to decipher this bullshit. And then the censor with his black pen, he redacts any word remaining that even faintly resembles the name of any poor bastard who recently died. The town is lost in all this. Soon there will be no need for a paper. There will be one word and nothing else. And these guys here, he said, pointing at the mourning mob taking the dead West northeast. It's... , he broke off, unable to find the words.

The nameless abomination, killing that within us that cannot be named, M quoted.

The mayor narrowed his eyes and looked at M sitting in the ute like a penitent, the newspaper in his lap. The mayor turned and spat and got out of the ute. His boots squelched on the already melting bitumen of morning.

The record of history, said M, unsure and not caring if the mayor could hear. That which was not reported did not occur, and what is unnamed never existed.

M picked up the newspaper and flattened it in his lap like smoothing out creases in bed sheets. He placed his hand at the top of the page to read the modern stone tablet by feel. As his finger moved, the shape of the inked letters absorbed into his fingertip. The letters of the incomprehensible headline formed slowly on his lips: KUMNJI-SLATOR KUMNJI-KUMNJI KUMNJI KUMNJI-KUMNJI. The occasional plain-English word appeared amid the destruction of a language. With deftness and an intimate knowledge of birth names he settled on the following translation: TRAN-SLATOR DES-LUCIFER KOOMANJAY TABATHA-LES. M said the phrase aloud. The mayor looked up. What did you say? M continued reading, his finger rushing across the sheet and returning, smudging the inky letters until at the end of the page the serrated edge cut. A drop of inky blood formed and fell and spread, slowly turning the page crimson.

Ow, M said. The wailing rose out of the earth again. M hummed.

Another death nearby, said M. Another nobody for that place ... the one, you know ... that, um...

M began to forget the names for things. That part of him—was it memory or knowledge?—became blurry and indistinct, a premonition that defied concentration. The named were becoming un- ... un-placed, unknown, purged. In his emerging vagueness the sound of a song grew in volume and intensity. He recognised snippets as those he had heard approaching the town this morning.

This was the unnameable song, the song of the town. It was all he now knew, all he needed to know.

As the life of M slowly bled out into the blotting paper, a tremor came over his lips as he chanted, silently, the words he would never be able to reveal. The unnameable names.

Om koomanjaya namaha.

[O Hail the Unnameable.]

Om koomanjai namaha.

[O Hail the Ineffable.]

Om koomanjay-koomanjaye namaha.

[O Hail the Word Made Mute.]

Om koomanjaya namaha ...

Revelations of Leonardo

There are moments in our youth when we are graded and sorted and marked, and our divine purpose is revealed. For the bastard son of Messer Piero Fruosino di Antonio da Vinci and the peasant Caterina, there were two such incidents of revelation.

The first occurred when he was still a babe in the cradle. An angel, taking the form of a kite hawk, plunged out of heaven to pay tribute. The hawk hovered over the cradle, and caressed the babe's face with the secret flapping of wings and the gentle brush of its tail feathers.

The second occurred some years later. Having wandered off alone in the mountains, he came to a dark cave. At the entrance he stopped. What unknown terrors or treasures were hidden inside? Two emotions fought within him: to flee, or to find out. Without thinking about what he was doing or what might happen to him, he stepped forward into the enveloping darkness.

These anecdotes, he observed later in his life, explained his unique gift for painting and sculpture, and his unstinting observation and investigation in all realms of art and science. But the anecdotes were also a mask for a third, undisclosed, revelation.

Throughout the summer nights of 1465, young Leonardo da Vinci had a recurring dream of an upstairs room at the end of a great corridor. The room was not empty. Large leather-bound books were stacked roughly in the shelves and in unstable towers on the floor. Novel objects made from unknown materials were suspended from the rafters and littered any surface free of books. In a small clearing on the desk a lantern burned. Beside it: a pitcher of wine, an inkpot, a quill. The leather cushion on the chair was comfortably compressed and still warm. Perhaps the occupant had been called away suddenly, urgently, and would return soon.

From that moment Leonardo committed himself to the labour of recall: to reproduce everything he observed and read in that visionary room during those long summer nights.

For this endeavour, he arranged and outfitted his study upstairs at the end of a long corridor in the same fashion as that which he remembered, including a seat with one short leg propped up by a wooden wedge. He stared at the mirror and obsessively copied out the reflections therein from the shadows of memory.

When Leonardo died, his notebooks numbered in the tens of thousands of pages. They covered his desk and crowded the shelves of his study. They rose in many columns from the floor. There were volumes dedicated to all realms of creation and their innermost workings. Fantastic diagrams, all diligently noted in his left-handed mirror-image script. The wings of birds; flying apparatus; the mechanics of the human body; the dissection of pregnant women; the butchery of unborn infants. And so much more.

And yet, despite his prolific output, this was merely a fragment, and quite possibly an imperfect fragment, of all that he had read and examined within his dream study. Perhaps Leonardo thought he had recalled it all, and recalled it all perfectly? Such is the vanity of gods and men.

In his lifetime, his work remained uncatalogued, poorly organised, and unpublished. For many feared that what Leonardo revealed in painstaking detail were the intricate designs of God whose logic is, and must remain, unfathomable, and any revelation of such was a grave desecration! His work, surely, could only be guided by the hand of Satan. (But then who is Satan if not an instrument of God?)

The final parchment on Leonardo's desk when he died was illegible. It was retained in a folder with other loose sheaves for completeness only. When a servant came to cleanse the room after the funeral, bent over a pile of notebooks, she bumped the desk and the pitcher of wine spilt and bled out over the page and the inky letters were swept away in the red river. It is only now, five hundred years later, using technology loosely inspired—some might say, prophesised—by Leonardo, that the ghost-like shadow of his final notes can be revealed.

The primary purpose of this analysis is to decipher the dissolved text from the wash of wine and ink. However, considering the nature of the restored text, further analysis was deemed prudent in order to determine the authenticity and attribution of said document. It must be stated that at no stage in over 500 years has the authorship of the document ever been disputed.

Carbon dating, and chemical and spectrum analysis of the paper, ink and wine were conducted and permission was granted to compare the results with samples taken from Leonardo's latter notebooks. The results of the separate analyses align perfectly, confirming that the ink and paper were of the same age and stock as that used by Leonardo.

> A symbol: *The letter Y bounded by a circle.*
> The text: *Designs for a new world by Yeshuah.*

The handwriting analysis, however, revealed a different style in the construction of letters and words.

Leonardo wrote with his left-hand. If he were to write from left to right (as is normal for the language) then he risked smudging the words already written with his trailing hand. To counter this, Leonardo wrote from right to left in a mirror-image flowing script that leant to the left. The resulting text seemed to be devilish incantations. However, viewed in a mirror, his notes were easily read and appeared as if they were written left to right with a right-leaning flowing script.

The examined text was written not in a flowing script, but letter by letter with intervening gaps. This style has not been observed in any of Leonardo's notebooks and writings.

The examined text was written from right to left, as evidenced by the placement of initial ink blobs (where the quill began to form a letter), the direction of ink flow in the construction of each letter, the location of the trailing tail, and by the degree of inclination of the letters in relation to the sentence line. However, under closer inspection, the examined text (A) appears not merely to have been written right to left in mirror-image, but *from the reflection* of a right to left mirror-image (A1) of the same text. It is even possible that this mirror-image (A1) is a reflection from not only a second mirror (A2), but from a third, or fourth, or n^{th} mirror. It is not possible using current technology—or even any currently imagined technology—to determine accurately the number of reflective iterations responsible.

In summary, while there are differences in the actual writing style, it is the view of this assessor that the examined text is most certainly by the hand of Leonardo, albeit given the actual text thus revealed, it is a copy of a copy of a copy (of a)…

Last drink

for Italo Svevo

Drink up, my friend, drink up, I'll shout another. They've just rung the bell for last drinks.

Here. Cheers! … Ah! A fine drop. Now I must tell you, my friend. I know a fellow, a patient of mine, let me see, is he here? he was here a short while ago. Anyway, this fellow likes to smoke, always a smoke on his lips, one to the next. But he is always giving up, he says. *This is my last cigarette* he says as he lights up, *This is my last cigarette* every time. Last cigarette, sure, we all nudge each other. And the rest of the packet in your pocket? He tells me in all confidence, *No-one takes me seriously, but as I trample the butt into the dust, I feel like I am trampling on my old ways and beginning anew without the burden of my mistakes.* True, he said that. And there was something, I don't know, something about the look that came over him when he said that, a radiant glow, like he was seeing an angel and I wasn't in the room with him at all.

Well, it got me to thinking. Now, I know there are some people that think that just because they see me in here everyday that I am an irredeemable alcoholic. *Look at your nose*, they say, *red and bulbous like a deformed beet*, as if that were all there was to being an alcoholic. Well, I like a drink I admit, just as much as the next man, but that fellow and the look that came over him, well, it got me to wondering where can I get a piece of that. The booze wasn't cutting it for me, no matter how heavy I hit it. So I decided to quit. I was sitting here, right here, in this bar. I ordered a tall beer. It arrived with a good head and beads of coolness ran down the side of the glass. It was a work of art, my friend, and I had a lust for it. So I took that fine ale in my hand and raised it high and announced *This is my last drink*. Some of the fellows cheered and drank up. I gulped down the golden nectar and slammed down the glass on the counter and gave an almighty belch. The bartender made to pull me another, but I waved him off, grabbed my coat and hat and pushed through the swinging door. And lo and behold, I floated down the cobbled streets, my shoes barely tapping the ground. I felt a rapture, as if all my encumbrances were being stripped away and I was created anew. Oh, I know what I must have looked like, singing and twirling, dancing and stumbling, making love to the alley cats and potted plants, tossing pennies into the fountain, I must have looked like some old drunken fool returning home late to a cold plate of herring and rye like so many times before, but it's not what we see that's important, it's what we feel, here, deep inside. I was drunk, yes, but not full drunk with drink, no my friend, I was drunk with the feeling of having given up drinking! And that new feeling of joy overwhelmed me so completely that I tingled all over. I felt as buoyant as a hot air balloon. As I passed by the corner store on R—— Street I caught my reflection in the window. My face glowed with a penumbra of light. I recalled paintings of saints and angels. And I recalled the face of that fellow who smoked his last cigarette. I stood and stared at my illumination and all the mistakes I had made, the wrong words I had said, the bad habits I had repeated, they all fell away and there in my heart beat the new me free of all that garbage. And I stood there humming blissfully for I don't know how long, minutes, hours, until a policeman came by and rapped me on the shoulder and told me to move on. When I awoke in the morning, the exhilarating feeling lingered like the tailings of a dream, a hangover in reverse. I sat at the kitchen table smiling until the coffee in front me went cold. I bathed and shaved and put on a new suit. I'm not sure what happened or how, but of one thing I was certain: I desperately needed that overwhelming bliss that held me last night after having my last drink. I would do anything and everything to feel that way again. Now, I like a drink my friend, but it's six of one and a half dozen of the other to me; it doesn't hold me. I'm not sitting here with you now to get drunk, no sir. I'm here for the euphoria of giving up drinking. So drink up, my friend, because this is my last drink.

Ah! Such bliss!

Good night, my friend. See you tomorrow at Café Italia. Oh, I can't wait! The first round is on me.

The forking path

A smudge of carbon
And a flicker of rust
Wandering through
A whirlwind of dust
Anonymous nursery rhyme, recollected during a
meditation

Her thin-soled shoes leave no prints on the rocky slab. *We pass through this life and our footsteps leave only a faint trail,* her teacher said, *a shallow gutter for others to follow and deepen.* To herself, to the rocks, she incants the phrase as she climbs the well-trodden path away from the bitumen and street lights towards the saddle between rocky knolls where shaggy hill-kangaroos doze in the indifferent shade of acacias, and beyond, into country lacking the landmarks of humanity.

This is my path, she declares. Who will sing it into being after me?

The train of her full-length dress swishes through the grass in response, gathering seeds and burrs in the thinning cotton. She advances like a faded version of fire. The original colour of the dress gathers in pockets, seen only when the stitching on a hem unravels and the rich colour spills into the light like meat ants erupting from their underground cells when disturbed. It is the colour of the rocks she tramples over, whose iron rust has leached to the surface, the colour of the marigolds which abound in her garden.

She follows the footpad intently, focusing on the placement of each step, aware of the muscle contractions around her ankle when an uneven rock moves, aware of the inconsistent camber of the slope.

Her dog is off ahead somewhere in the sparse scrub of the indistinct hills and gullies, sniffing the grasses and scats, and lifting a leg to re-announce his presence. The dog always returns to her, finding her scent on a kicked stone or a bush that she has brushed past.

Many years ago she got lost out here amid the undulating hills and scrappy trees and quartz outcrops that all look the same. In her inexperience and panic, she did not think to track her own footsteps back or allow the dog to lead. Hours she spent, zigzagging through what appeared to be familiar terrain and then wasn't, until finally she emerged on a recently bulldozed track that eventually returned her home as dusk settled and she had no idea where she had ventured or what direction she had taken. But that was before she found this one path through the wilderness, the one she has followed devotedly without deviation for years, keeping it clear by tossing aside loose stones and the debris of fallen trees and limbs, cropping branches that strive towards open space and impede her progress.

She stops suddenly at the threshold. She stands with one foot on rusted earth, the other on ash. She has seen images, but she is unprepared for the actuality of lived experience. Behind her everything is green and alive; ahead stretches a black canvas patchily dotted in gobs of green. She gasps. She has been away for weeks. This is her first time walking her path since returning from some tests in a distant city, the first time since the fires.

A friend patrolled the hills during those days and nights of fire, uploading shaky videos to Facebook. From a hospital bed one thousand miles away with a tube hydrating her body, she repeatedly braved the heat and smoke and ash to walk vicariously with fire as it painted the country—her country—black.

Fire came like a distant relative that you once invited out of politeness, saying 'come visit ... we have a spare room' without any intention of them ever taking up the offer. Yes, fire came and walked against the flow of air and wind into your life and with its hot breath ingratiated itself into your home. It left unwashed dishes, and pizza cartons on the lounge room floor for a finger-thick trail of ants to clean. It drank the last of the full-cream milk without replenishing or leaving a note, and you were forced to make powdered skim with shaky hands for your morning coffee. It ate the entire block of decadent chocolate you had stashed behind the red lentils. It camped in the lounge watching DVDs all day. It was there when you left for work in the morning, still there when you came home. Not offering to make dinner—just there. Always there. There with a question, ten questions, when you just wanted silence and solitude. And that's how the fire came over the hill and marched through the grass and shrubs—like it was its right to do as it pleased.

Yes, fire came and walked against the flow of air and wind consuming oxygen and organic matter, trailing its black cloak over the roasted earth. It crept like a tortoise against the breeze, unflinching in its determination. It embraced the dry grasses with passion. It ignited trees like incandescent candles, their waxy leaves exploding in fire-bombs.

She watched the flaming scenes over and over, breathing in time with the fire's lurching progress. The cigarette trailing from her lips glowed, each inhalation in time with the crescendo of fire and air and fuel. Fuel—such a strange way to think of living trees now turned to ash to compost the earth. But it would regrow, given time. And burn again. The cycle was endless. But was it spiralling upwards, burning and cleansing, removing impurities to become a greater form, pure and hard as a diamond? Or spiralling downwards, destroying everything of value, bit by little bit, wearing it down to expose the sludge at its worthless core?

Several years ago, after having walked the path in the same direction thousands of times—yes, thousands: twice a day, at dawn and near dusk—a friend joked that she must be able to walk it blindfolded. She was intrigued by the notion, that every step and turn, each twist and sway of body to avoid a protruding rock or overhanging branch, could be ingrained into her unconsciousness and the walk could be a dance between her and the path. She tried a few times, but she stubbed a toe on a rock she had not noticed before or walked headlong into a golden orb web that she normally passed by. She told a fellow student about how she had recently fallen on a clump of spinifex while walking blindly and was still getting the embedded points out of her hand and thigh. Her teacher overheard and interrupted: *Our every act and our every moment must be lived consciously, otherwise there is no benefit.* After that lesson she resolved to walk with full sensorial awareness, to feel the imprint and shape of every stone on her sole.

Now she walks with new conviction, taking in an environment recast by fire. She marvels at the differences in a landscape that had seemed as familiar to her as the mantra she chants by rote. Obliterated of many of their shrubs and grasses, the low hills expose themselves as overlapping rocky scales tilted from the horizontal. Further on there are rock scatters she has never seen before. Flakes of white quartz on the orange-red-black earth look like exquisite mosaics of master tilers, or the many-brush-stroked foreground of a Rod Moss painting. Blackened bowls in rock slabs where rain collects temporarily before evaporating, and quartz veins that glisten like marbled fat. Beside a rocky crest, she follows a low wall of boulders that appears to have been hastily erected against a horde and quickly abandoned, the 'wall' remaining more as an expression of intent that an actual defiance, easily stepped over, which she does. There are places where the path had been thickly overgrown by feral grasses, but those grasses are now blackened stumps and the path revealed is as deeply ingrained as an addiction.

In the devastated landscape, more paths appear. Roo pads, some very well used, link sand scrapes like lines connecting circular nodes on a transport map; some are distinct for a step or two before entering rocky ground where their direction is intuited only by the marsupial's preference for linear bounds.

In clear ground that now invites uninhibited walking, her path dog-legs around phantom objects. But she does not deviate. She follows her old path meticulously, taking the kinks around former bushes or the remains of a fence. She meanders through open country as if the burnt shrubs are still present and she has to prune the protruding fronds with the secateurs in her pocket. Through a stand of blackened witchetty bushes she passes. The hardened branches, tougher in death than in life, streak her dress with black stripes like a thylacine (whose hills she can see occasionally to the west).

Her path, with much of its familiarity obliterated, seems to her both new and old. In several places she loses her way. She knows that she can be only one step or two away from the path, or even standing on it but looking away from the line of travel, and not see it. Sometimes, she says to herself, you don't see it until you are moving along it, as if it doesn't exist without someone walking it into being.

Eventually she walks into an open flat where formerly a stand of corkwood trees whispered. It is her favourite section along the path, a place where she often sits in the communal shade and meditates, her dog stretched out nearby like a sphinx. The corkwoods are wizened grandmothers: soft and dark and deeply fissured, their every inch of growth squeezed and twisted over decades, their long needled fingers curling upwards. She knows people in town who have bought their house almost solely because of the old-lady corkwood in the yard.

She stops, rolls and lights a cigarette, and draws greedily.

This is the sight that sears her mind. This is the canvas she will paint later: coal black smeared roughly onto black that is gouged deeply in the shape of trees up-ended then filled with a fine grey the colour and texture of bleached and burnt bone.

The corkwoods have been incinerated in-situ. Their grey ash shrouds remain as ghostly reminders, like the chalked outline of the dead on bitumen, leaving a fine porous powder where nothing will regrow. And here fire is still at work, creeping like gangrene along the severed limb, slowly consuming all living flesh, to where the arthritic fingers of one branch remain.

She takes a deep draw. The burnt tobacco is a long ash cylinder before breaking off at her feet. She smokes the cigarette to just before the filter, then with yellow-stained fingers the colour of dead-finish arils, puts the butt in a small metal tin. When the tin nears full, she will deposit a small cairn of the contents in a local park to be collected and resurrected into a new cigarette by others.

She bends to the smouldering branch, lifts it clear of the warm ash shroud then places it on the blackened earth, just beyond the reach of burning death.

What will my remnants be? she thinks. And: How will they be of use to others?

She rolls another then walks on. At a place in low hills where the path is indistinct she stops beside a dead witchetty bush whose root base has been incinerated totally, leaving a rounded divot of grey ash, a small foxhole, a grenade blast. The dead limbs fan out on the ground from the burnt core like a dress unzipped, dropped to a lover's floor, and stepped out of. The central circle of ash anoints the earth like the ash tikka on her forehead, placed there this morning at the weekly fire ceremony. The vibhuti. The sacred ash burnt in sacred fire while chanting Sanskrit mantras, a symbol of the purifying fire with which Lord Shiva, the auspicious one, burnt Desire to ashes. It reminds her, as she licks the paper then lights up, of the grey smudge the doctor pointed out on her scan.

Hints of green regrowth break the darkened soil nearby.

The weeds first, she thinks. Everything in the body dies. Except cancer. It is regrowth.

Unconsciously, she cups the familiar weight of her breast in a curved hand, still inhaling. She watches her shadow hand holding her shadow breast, and she feels the weight of her shadow increasing with the sinking sun. You could be a diver yet, she jokes to herself, once this ballast is removed.

Around the flattened, fanned-out bush she walks, smoking one then another. After several circumambulations, she stops. Looks up. Looks around. Turns and scuffs the ground. Steps and turns and scuffs again.

Oh, shit, she says aloud, where is the path?

There are many pilgrims on many paths, her teacher said in her first lesson. *They shout to each other as they walk along: 'You are going the wrong way. Come here and join me. For this is the right path.' They stop and harangue each other, or waste effort by jumping from this path to that, trying it out like a costume before discarding it for another, and then another. They dabble without progress because of their ignorance.*

This is the truth: All paths lead to the one.

This one. That one. Their one.

Choose a path that feels right for you. Then commit to it fully: mind, body and soul. Commit yourself to the service of it.

She turns and turns but doesn't know where she is. The markers gone. The path lost. Animal pads spear off in many directions. Where is her path, the right path?

Does it matter which she takes? They all lead somewhere. But this enters her mind only as anxiety, not as an option. She can backtrack to a known point then continue forward again. But in all her turning she has scuffed her shoe prints senseless and she doesn't recognise any landmark in the obliterated distance that she could aim for.

Her dog is a few metres away, panting after a chase, but still listening for the thunk of a kangaroo springing on rock, always ready to sprint off again no matter how tired. She looks to the dog for assistance, but any essence of their past scent has been burnt away. There is only now.

So she stands still and closes her eyes, then turns and turns and turns, and when she stops chanting she stops turning, opens her eyes and looks straight ahead. She takes some seconds to recover from the vertigo.

She takes a step.

(Hesitantly or boldly, you decide.)

The dog is at her side. She takes another step. And another.

(Divide yourselves into two camps.)

Right after left, or right leading left.

(Sub-divide repeatedly and mutate.)

She knows not if this is the same path or another …

(Argue among yourselves whichever way.)

… but she continues, she continues walking on.

Minister for Lost

L ast month, sometime and somewhere between leaving for work in the early morning and arriving home in the gathering sunset, the Minister for Lost went missing.

His secretary could neither confirm nor deny that he had, in fact, been at work. The previous day, the Minister for Lost had informed her that tomorrow he would be in meetings all day, that he did not want to be disturbed, no ifs or buts.

She arrived for work on time. She saw the minister's overcoat and hat on the rack. His office door was closed. At times she heard voices and muffled laughter coming from the office, but she could not clearly distinguish his among them. When she left the office at 6 pm, his office door had not opened all day and his hat and overcoat had not been touched. The next morning when she arrived they were not there, and though one month had now passed, they had not reappeared.

Pictures of people's faces, their name, age, and location last seen. They flash by on the television screen during the daily missing persons report immediately prior to the evening newscast. If you have seen or have information about any of these people then please call this number.

The (newly appointed) Minister for Lost arrives early for his first day. As he closes the door of his office behind him he feels a little lighter, as if the burden of the new ministry has diminished already with this single act. He moves to his desk and sits and grabs the desk diary. He opens it, but for the moment he has forgotten today's date. Out of habit he puts a hand in his right trouser pocket, then the other side, then with a slight scowl, pats his chest pocket, and then scrunches the outer and inner pockets of his jacket. What have I done with that bloody phone this time? he says to no-one.

He searches his briefcase. No phone. He calls his mobile with the office landline. No pulsing or vibration can be heard or felt. Bugger, he says, I must have left it on the mantel again; never mind.

The Minister grabs today's newspaper from his case. He finds today in the desk diary. No appointments. He turns the page to tomorrow. No appointments. And the next day, and the next. For weeks and months ahead, all the pages are blank.

What do they do here? he asks himself. What am I meant to do here?

He had imagined that the job would be fulfilling. Receiving and registering letters and calls and emails from people for all manner of missing things: lost cats, lost dogs, lost socks, lost pens, lost memories, lost childhoods, lost dreams, lost parents, lost desires, lost moments, lost loves, lost lives. They would be recorded and noted. They would be stamped with his seal. They would be indexed and filed away.

Lost.

It was not the responsibility of the Minister for Lost to go out and find what had been reported as being lost. Long ago that role had been given to the Ministry for Found, whose minister at that time was making a power grab within government. Previously, the

Ministry for Found recorded and indexed the details and location of found objects around the state. But the Minister for Found thought they could provide a better service to the electorate (and in doing so, increase his public profile and popularity, and correspondingly, increase his chances of ousting the incumbent prime minister). And so the Ministry for Found hired more agents and sent them out to retrieve the found objects and return them to a centralised depot for collection. More agents were hired and sent out to find lost objects. Some items were found before they had been reported lost, and some items had not even been lost.

As the number of uncollected found items increased, the Ministry for Found began to resemble an opportunity shop, albeit on the scale of a multi-level warehouse, with items stacked in avenues of shelves that reached to the ceiling, and clerks wearing hi-vis vests, steel-cap boots and yellow helmets driving forklifts up and down the grid.

At an emergency meeting of government, the Ministry for Found requested access to the vast records and databases of the Ministry for Lost, but there were strident objections relating to privacy and data integrity. Instead, the Ministry for Found launched a marketing campaign for a 24-hour info-channel to advertise and display the found items so the populace could watch and see and come in to collect their lost and found items.

More and more found items arrived hourly by the pallet load. Trucks queued at the unloading bay. Ships queued at the docks. And it seemed the entire population of the country came to look for the things they had lost, watching on the big screen erected in the plaza outside the ministry building, hoping that their lost items might be among those collected by the Ministry for Found. They pushed through windows and doors. Some people fell. They were trampled into mush. Still people kept pushing to get in. The army was called. In the end, the solution demanded by a raving Minister for Found standing on the roof of his ministry was to bomb the building. The government was not willing to fire upon its own people for fear of bad press. Instead, they ordered a secret service agent posing as an airline steward on a passenger airplane to take control of the cockpit, divert, and fly into the building. Terrorists could be blamed.

The Ministry for Found was lost, irrevocably. But that was long ago. The rubble of the building was converted into a park. Found objects were excavated and amalgamated into sculptures in the centre of the park. No-one came to claim them.

So the new Minister for Lost sets himself to work. He pats the chest pocket of his business shirt for a pen. He opens the top right drawer of the desk and rummages inside. Then likewise the left. He makes a mental note to get a pen. He buzzes his secretary.

The Minister for Lost looks up. Across the room, a few paces inside the door, there stands a young woman, not unattractive, sensibly attired in a feminine way, her full attention on him, pen and pad poised. He didn't hear her enter. He doesn't know how long she has been standing there. He doesn't recognise who she is.

She has seen his blank look on the faces of many men. She feels some disquiet, but only momentarily.

Ahem, she says softly, raising a hand to cover her mouth. Ahem.

She sees dust motes fall like rain between them. She sees his eyes twitch slightly. Ahem, she says a final time.

With no response, she turns and walks out the room, his eyes following her, closing the door behind her.

How many times has he wished that his son and daughter, his mother-in-law, his brother, and his wife – yes especially his wife – would just leave him be? How many times has he wished, how many times today even, has he wished that they would go and get lost? What does that phrase really mean? Get lost. And get found again? Or remain lost? And lost from whom or what? Just from him? From others? From God? What would that be like? If you really knew, would you wish it on anyone?

He begins to think about all of the things that he has ever lost. What they were. When and where they were last used. What they meant to him. What they mean to him now. With this subtle observation he realises that they are not lost at all, that he has found them within himself.

A half-smile stretches the face of the Minister for Lost. His mobile phone buzzes with an incoming message. He grabs the pen beside the pile of correspondence on his desk. He opens the letter on top of the pile with a blade, puts on his reading glasses, and finds his work.

Six days and nights beneath the Bodhi Tree

If a man watches not for nirvana
his cravings grow like a creeper
and he leaps from death to death
like a monkey in the forest
from one tree without fruit to another.
Dhammapada 334

First day

I sit cross-legged on the white marble tiles in meditation pose, sukhasana. My eyes are closed, my arms extended. The backs of my open hands are on my knees; the index fingers bend over and bow to the thumb in chinmudra, stimulating the union of my outer self with the inner self.

I sit beneath the Mahabodhi Tree whose branches reach up to heaven, whose roots protrude across all Asia. I invoke the calm resolve of granite. And I recall the deeds of Siddhartha Gautama, a prince of the Shakya clan, who 2,500 years ago renounced his kingdom, his wife, his children, and a life of material comfort in order to find liberation from the cycle of suffering: birth, life, illness, death and rebirth. Six harsh years of ascetic piety reduced him to a living skeleton, but still he was tainted by craving and aversion. Finally, at the foot of this very same banyan tree where I now sit, he sat with an unshakable vow:

> Here on this seat my body may shrivel up, my skin, my bones, my flesh may dissolve, but I will not move from this very seat until I attain enlightenment.

On that full moon night his mind was opened—irrevocably. His wisdom became total. He became a Buddha, an Awakened One, and flowers rained from the heavens.

I sit with steely intent.

Within minutes my feet are numb. My mind leaps between sounds, thoughts and opinions. A fly disturbs the hairs on my forearm. An itch tickles my nose. My lower back aches. With effort I pull the cross of my legs apart and grimace as the blood flow shockingly returns. I massage the tingling limb. I rue my lack of discipline and commitment.

After a time, I rise and stumble away. Four words tag along with me: ignorance, suffering, craving, aversion. Outside the temple, I take a seat at a roadside dhaba and order chai and samosa.

Second day

I decide to perform six clockwise koras of the Mahabodhi Tree and Temple before sitting and meditating. On the first lap, a small dry curled-up leaf waits on the marble tiles behind a seated group. I pick it up and continue. On the second kora, a perfectly formed heart-shaped leaf falls one pace in front of me. An offering for me. I smile and pick it up without breaking stride. I hold it in utmost respect to my forehead and heart. And then complete the remaining koras.

I sit beneath the western fringe of the sacred banyan tree, whose propped-up limbs spread a network of shade over the temple's outer courtyard. Beneath the canopy, hundreds of Buddhist flags, vertically striped blue-yellow-red-white-orange, traverse and criss-cross. The scene is at once sensorial, spiritual and symbolic.[1] A golden temple dog, male, with dingo-like features, lies down beside me and rests his head against my thigh. He sleeps a while. I look up at the many birds going about their autumnal business. The dog leaves then later returns unbidden to sleep in the same position.

In the Sadgatikārikā, the Buddhist poet Dhārmika Subhūti describes the karmic reasons for the rebirth of sentient beings as animals. The dog resting on my thigh is in this life a dog due to haughtiness, an arrogantly superior and disdainful self-importance; he is unperturbed by a pat on the head or nose, a scratch on the chin. Pigeons, who in a former life could not forgo a passionate attachment to sensual pleasures, flit through the branches above. The squawking of mynas and parrots and woodpeckers is incessant. Squirrels dart along branches for small fruits. The relentless activity of all these sentient beings shakes twigs and fruit and leaves from the tree.

Beneath the branches, monks and lay disciples collect the fallen organic matter. The most highly prized are the heart-shaped leaves. They serve as an organic relic of the tree's spiritual power and an inspiration to all who seek a release from suffering.

But this is not the exact same banyan tree, *Ficus religiosa*, of Buddha, even though it has the same DNA. Around 250 BCE, the wife of the great Indian emperor Ashoka poisoned the tree because her husband paid more attention to the Buddhist teachings, the Dharma, than he did to her. The tree apparently died, then regrew from the base. Shortly before the poisoning, Ashoka's daughter took a cutting of the sacred tree to be planted in Sri Lanka where it still lives. A cutting from the Lankan tree was returned to India

---

1. The colours of the flags represent the rings of the aura that visibly surrounded Buddha's head after attaining enlightenment. Blue is for universal compassion, yellow for the middle way between asceticism and worldly attachment—neither denying nor craving, red for blessings, white for purity and liberation, and orange for wisdom.

in 1881 to replace the original tree that appeared to be dying of old age.

I approach two monks in the earth-brown-coloured robes of Thai Buddhists. They have been collecting twigs and leaves from the tree. One of the monks notices the red string around my neck.

'You are Buddhist?'

He draws the string from beneath my shirt and studies the mandala necklet. Out of a small bag he takes an irregular golden cylinder two inches long and tied with two braids of red-black and gold-black cord. He points at the tree. I infer that encased in the gold wrapper is a twig from the Bodhi Tree. But is the gold wrapper real gold beaten thin as foil (like that stuck on Buddha images throughout Burma) or from a Cadbury chocolate block? He ties the offering on to my red string necklet.

The other monk holds up a bag of twigs he has collected then displays a delicate wooden artefact, smaller than a thumbnail and only millimetres thick. With patient detail, the monk carves the Bodhi twigs into miniature Buddha icons. He places one in my palm. It reminds me that it is the tree that gives, that man must reconnect with nature, not be removed from it or enclose himself in buildings of cement and brick. I hold the treasured gift up to my forehead and to my heart then put it in my pocket for my protection.

Second night

I enter at dusk with a throng of pilgrims. In the trees, the birds settle noisily. Beneath them, pilgrims of many nationalities gather in separate groups for ceremonial prayers in their own language: Malay, Burmese, Thai, Sinhalese, Japanese, Korean, Taiwanese, and more. Further out in the garden, some Tibetan monks have a light dinner while others prepare for their physical-spiritual workout: a sweaty session of prostrations (a cross between burpees and prayer) while reciting a mantra for humility as an antidote to pride.

I ascend the stairs to the standing-gazing spot, where Buddha spent the second week after attaining enlightenment contemplating the tree with grace and gratitude. From here now, except for some outer branches, the temple commands the view and the tree is no longer visible. I contemplate change, and impermanence.

Third night

A festive atmosphere pervades the market as locals shop for sweets and candles, toy guns and fireworks and icons for Diwali, the Festival of Lights, a major Hindu festival. Over several days that have many meanings, Diwali celebrates the triumph of good over evil when Lord Krishna killed the demon Narakasura, and it also welcomes the return of the prodigal son, Ram, hero of the epic Ramayana, after fourteen years of exile. Windows and trees are lit with candles; fireworks, loud noise and distorted music keep evil spirits at bay; sweets are shared; and everyone dresses in new clothes. The home is cleaned thoroughly to honour and welcome Lakshmi, goddess of wealth and prosperity, and to seek her blessing. It is an occasion as important as Christmas is to Christians, as the Jewish Passover, as Tibetan Losar or Chinese New Year, and as Eid al-Fitr at the end of fasting month of Ramadan is to Muslims.

In their new clothes, thousands of people visit temples and pray for wealth and health, make offerings, and give alms to beggars. Through the temple gates they file between competing wants: a line of beggars and begging bowls and physical deformities on one side, and on the other, popcorn vendors and mala wallahs and icons for the home shrine.

But Diwali is not just bang and sparkle, there is a deeper significance.

The light. Diwali symbolises the awareness of our own inner light. The victory of good over evil—Krishna overpowering the demon—refers to the light of a higher knowledge dispelling the ignorance that masks our transcendental self. This awakening can bring a new sense of compassion, awareness and joy.

With this in mind, I take time to analyse my moral self. My thoughts and deeds today, have they been virtuous? And those unvirtuous thoughts, how can I circumvent them and act differently when they arise again? They are deeply imprinted in my brain, so they will surely arise again, maybe later today, maybe in a fortnight. What's done is done, but they will come again. And when they do, how do I propose to act? The answer to this lies along the meandering path beyond knowledge that leads to wisdom. But if I were to merit a human rebirth, my thoughts and actions today, at best, would have me return in servitude.

There is a very long queue at the temple's main gate. I dislike crowds, especially the jostling masses of humanity in India. The incessant tooting of horns shout at each other 'I'm here, I'm coming through', even in a traffic jam where no-one is moving and no-one is listening. Still the car horns scream. On foot, crowds push into a crush from behind, the push demanding 'I'm here, I want to get through' even when the crowd in front has been forced to stop. The pressure of self-importance and self-preservation is overwhelming. It is this human congestion that typifies India for me. This time I opt out and sit on the steps at the temple's locked north gate. Alone.

One hour later, after the sunset crush-hour, I enter and sit on a concrete platform just beyond the Bodhi Tree's canopy on the south-west side of the temple. I sit in sukhasana. I take my mala in my right hand to do a full round, 108 repetitions, of the Mahamrityunjaya mantra, a Sanskrit chant for health and healing. My voice blends with others chanting in the garden. Mosquitoes bite me several times, especially in the fleshy crook of the elbow. I open my eyes and swipe at them, trying not to kill them. I do not cease chanting. But I struggle to maintain a sense of ease. I refocus my attention at the eyebrow centre and complete the mala in twenty minutes.

At the moment I open my eyes, the golden dog from yesterday barrels into me and rolls playfully in my lap. I give him a pat and a rub behind the ears.

Fourth day

I sleep terribly, waking many times. I feel as if I am stuck in a queue going nowhere until the bell tolls 6 am. I rise, intending to visit the tree early, but my head spins and buzzes, and my brain bounces around like I am in a title fight entering the fifteenth round.

I go downstairs and sit on the outside steps of the Karma Temple and listen to the morning Tibetan puja: the low moaning chant, the blast of conch shell, the ringing bells, and the insistent drumming. I hack up phlegm into the garden. I return to my room and lie down. Hours pass. My head burns with fever, my lower back and kidneys ache. My chest and belly heave in waves, ridding muck. The day passes like a month. I don't go beyond the bathroom.

Crackers and bombs explode late into the night as if the city is under siege. Just over a week ago, six people were killed in Patna, the state capital, when eight pressure-cooker bombs exploded at a political rally. And only three months ago here in Bodhgaya, five people were injured when nine blasts rocked the Mahabodhi Temple. Security was increased. Bag searches, metal detectors, pat downs. But how are a few duty police with rifles supposed to thwart religious terrorism? When an explosion occurs, how do they separate a security threat from a child's cracker? Do they rely on the screams of the injured? The flow of blood? With the poor lighting and frequent power failures, I am surprised that the sale of crackers and toy guns is not altogether banned.

Fifth day

Modern molecular physics agrees with the ancient spiritual sciences of the East—we are merely energy fields vibrating in or out of rhythm with the world around us.

Sound waves are vibrations too. The sounds coming from outside the temple are mostly unnatural and stress-inducing: horns honking; engines revving and droning; Hindi-pop with its up-tempo bass, overly-lush strings and squawking soprano. Inside the temple grounds, the evening calls of pigeons and myna birds, and the chanting of monks and pilgrims, create a more soothing vibration, one that is conducive to quiet contemplation, reflection and meditation.

Both sages of old and modern yogis agree—that a person's thoughts and actions changes that person's subtle energy fields, thus changing the frequency at which they vibrate. And the frequency of these vibrations can also be altered by the chanting and repetition of mantra, which creates a specific vibrational harmony in the body. So it said in my light, metaphysical reading. In particular, the vibration created by the repetition of the Mahamrityunjaya mantra 108 times—which I recited two nights ago—activates manipura chakra, the life force at the solar plexus. By altering the body's internal vibration, the mantra stimulates the release of toxins from the physiological structure so that they can be purged and healing can take place.

Sixth day

Having wasted so much of my forty-plus years in non-spiritual endeavours, I sit this final day, considering the rare blessing of being born human and in a time and place where I am able to receive Buddha's teaching. I aspire to emulate Buddha and the path of awakening: I seek to gain knowledge of all of my past lives; and I seek to gain knowledge of karma, the law of cause and effect that conditions the universe, whereby everything that arises has a cause. I aspire to gain all of this, not as a theory, but as a lived experience; not merely as knowledge, but as active wisdom. For knowledge of its own accord is useless. It is only when knowledge is, through practical application and experience, metamorphosed into wisdom that it has any benefit.

My thoughts and actions—the cause—create or effect imprints in my brain. The more I do something, the greater the imprint. Like a well-trodden path. Like the passage of a river. If the cause— the thought or action—is removed, there is no effect. The circuit is defused. Apply this concept to all the causes of suffering: ignorance, attachment, aversion. If I can stay neutral, like a piece of wood, in the face of wants and needs and fears, then suffering cannot arise. When Siddharta experienced this wisdom, it completely destroyed the final traces of attachment and aversion and ignorance in his mind. This is nirvana. This is bliss. This is the experiential wisdom of Buddha.

After many weeks of contemplation, Buddha gave his first teaching. He espoused the Four Noble Truths: that life—the cravings and aversions through our actions, thoughts, and feelings—is suffering (because they don't satisfy us endlessly); that seeking more existence or experience is suffering (because, once again, they don't satisfy us endlessly); that forsaking passion by remaining neutral or equanimous in all things ceases suffering; and this equanimity is achieved through the eight-fold path of liberation: right view, right intention, right effort, right action, right livelihood, right speech, right mindfulness, and right meditation. This is the way.

It is early morning. There is fervent activity throughout the temple grounds. Two nuns make slow prostrating circuits of the temple. While repeatedly chanting their mantra, they bow in prayer head to foot. As they stretch bodily forward on the ground and extend their arms fully ahead of them, a piece of cloth covering the robe rises to shroud each face from the dust. Their gloved hands mark the spot to where their feet will shuffle forward for the next prostration. The birds are quiet.

I want to sit as close to the tree as possible. I want to feel the thrum of the tree's throbbing energy while there is silence and few other pilgrims are about.

I sit in accomplished pose, siddhasana, right hand laid atop the left in my lap, thumbs touching in dhyana mudra for meditation. I am north of the Bodhi Tree, about ten metres distant. A monk is within the inner locked enclosure that surrounds the tree and the place where Buddha sat. He passes out leaves and accepts offerings for the throne. Flower chains made up of orange and yellow marigolds are draped over the top of the gold foil-encrusted granite fence; fresh pink lotus flowers line the alcoves in the masonry below. The flowers, so beautiful when freshly cut, will wilt before the day ends.

From where I sit I can see the tree fully. The base rises from the raised earth, the many trunks twisting into major branches, and I follow one branch as it evolves into a minor branch that passes directly over my head.

I sit.

I sit in stillness.

When my meditation ends I bring my hands together, like a temple, a lotus, or a heart, thumbs within. I raise this offering to my forehead, to my throat, and to my heart. I bow forward with humility. My forehead presses against the marble tile. And still sitting, I rise.

Light shines on the upper branches. A new day has begun.

My eyes are open.

My hands are open.

Rats

From the flooding dark belowdecks, they come. Rats emerge en masse from piss-marked passages. Clawing and clamouring over timber and flesh. Rats spew forth from the lightless confines containing bilge and dank rot. Scratching and straining. Rats erupt from the thin veneer of pitch that was their sole protection from the crush of salt water inches away. Gnashing and squealing. Rats leap, without hesitation, into the roiling sea.

Fear has brought them to this point, falling through air. Their fear of water. Their fear of drowning.

Leaping. Falling.

Some don't survive the initial slap of the sea. Some gulp salt water and sink. Some are taken by fishes, some by gulls. Few resurface. Their unwebbed feet thrash with little effect; their muzzles barely pierce the water's surface and they gasp for solid air.

They don't see the ship roll and go under, but they feel the deep sea tug at their tails with its heavy sinking weight. Some go under. Those that fear most keep on thrashing.

And then the accursed ghost ship H.M.S. *Antaeus* breaches the surface like a humpback whale and lolls upon the calming sea. The ship has not sunk, and it is clear, even to the rats, that the ship will not sink. But they have abandoned her; neither the earnest pleas of Noah for one pair of rats to clamber aboard, nor the offer of limitless food and clean straw for bedding, could entice any of the rats to return to the ship. Instead they paddle, grasp and scratch, and clamber upon floating timbers. Their fur is a wet mat. Their chests heave.

Small waves emanating from the resurfacing ship push the driftwood towards the shore of the nearby island mountain, where on the rock-tossed shore the waves exhaust themselves. Beyond the strand, a grassy skirt inclines steadily to the base of a sheer cliff that rises from the island pedestal like a colossal column of an ancient temple whose scale cannot be comprehended, pushing up into a heavy layer of cloud that cloaks completely the upper steeps and terraces of Mt Purgatory.

The bloated corpses of shipwrecked sailors drift into the shallows where they bob just beyond the breakers. Even in death, the sailors are denied permission to make a landing on the sanctified shore. Their sorrowful souls have already fled elsewhere.

The rats squeal with hunger. Again, their instinct overcomes fear.

They jump into the warm sea. They swim and crawl aboard the dead rafts. The rats eat first the lips and tongue, then the eyes. They climb through passages to eat the brain, the stomach, the heart and liver and kidneys. They gnaw the fleshy limbs from the extremities back to the spine. They eat until the skeleton is clean and begins to sink. Then move on to the next corpse.

There are no other predators on the island, no other living beings. Be fruitful and multiply, says the Lord, conferring his blessing on the smartest of animals. Their offspring soon covers the meadow encircling the island from the rocky shore to the base of the cliffs. As sentient beings whose arteries still course with oxygenated blood, they are not permitted—and at any rate they are unable— to scale the *via ferrata* up the vertiginous cliff that leads to Saint

Peter's Gate, nor to see or know what is above the permanent layer of cloud.

But the Lord is pleased with the arrival of the rats, for this moment was foretold by the prophets of yore, even by David, so it is said. The rats gather at the strand, the landing place for the arrival of new penitents, as they have been instructed. A kite hawk drops from the enveloping cloud and snatches one of the rats in its talons. It hovers above the squealing rats. It pecks once at the forehead of the snared rat. Then drops it.

The rat twists in the air and lands like a cat. The rats press forward. Other than the drop of blood welling on its forehead, the chosen rat is unharmed. As the rats' whiskers touch the chosen rat, a bloody stigma marks their foreheads too. And soon all the rats are so marked.

When the next flying boat of an hundred penitent souls arrives, the rats are ready for their divine mission. For the Lord is fond of testing the mettle of Its people, as Its servant Job will readily testify. So when the hundred souls as one leap ashore at the base of Mt Purgatory, innocent as a boatload of refugees washing up on a foreign shore, the rats attack.

These souls are not living people, but being so recently dead they often forget that they are no longer alive. As shades who are yet to pass through St Peter's Gate, from whence their many years or decades—and in some extreme cases, centuries—of inner cleansing of the root causes of sin will commence, they are still capable of feeling every human emotion and physical torment. And their waking dreams can still dissolve into limitless nightmares.

The rats attack the shades, swarming over them. Before the shades can turn around or scream they are covered from head to foot in rat coats sewn together with powerful jaws and ripping teeth. Gnash, shred, flesh, entrails. The screaming and wailing is almost hellish. (Praise the Lord, one shade says to another as they pass through the thick layer of cloud that screens the upper peak from earthly view. The cloud band is soundproof. Amen to that, the other shade replies.)

Many shades, covered by their coat of many hells, stagger away in slow motion as if they wear lead-weighted boots. They stumble and roll, but no manner of thrashing about can remove the gnawing coat of rats from them. Some shades emerge from the affray with a tattered rat coat, ripping the remaining threads from themselves and throwing them in the direction of the sea as they canter up the slope towards the cliff, correctly intuiting that their salvation begins there. And then there are the very few, perhaps only one shade, no more, per boatload: the pure of heart and intention, who float through the plague of rats as if they are arm in arm with their dearest beloved, strolling without any worldly cares through a field of sunflowers on a sunny summer Sunday.

The uncoupling of Eduardo Martinez

What you are is what you have been,
what you will be is what you do now.
  Buddha

1.

Midway through the afternoon class, the police constable, cap in hand, tapped lightly on the schoolroom door and entered without waiting for a reply. He closed the door quietly behind him then stood, facing the class, shifting his weight from one foot to the other. Between him and the ragged pupils the aged schoolmaster stood, leaning his wiry frame against the front of his desk. On the faded blackboard behind the schoolmaster, chalked in his neatest script, was a single underlined word: <u>GENEALOGY.</u>

The schoolmaster was unaware that someone had entered the room—only the eyes of his few students, drawn to the rocking statue of the uniformed visitor, alerted him. As he turned his head, the schoolmaster concluded the spoken lesson about the transference of dominant and regressive genes during selective breeding: 'So, by carefully selecting the parent animals or flowers for specific qualities, we can produce an offspring that is a hybrid, a new strain, one that is genetically different, superior even, to its creators.' As he spoke, he signalled to the constable to come forward, and as the final word echoed around the hollow room, the constable whispered into his ear.

Less than one minute later, the constable, cap on head, was striding out the school gate closely tailed by the young student, Eduardo Martinez, who had to alternately walk, skip, and trot to keep pace. They soon came to the major avenue busy with cars, buses, and trucks, all heading elsewhere: to the airport, the city, everywhere but here.

The other side of the avenue was a deserted stretch of low scrub. In the distance, shimmering in the heat haze, lay the metal tracks of the railway. Neither spoke while they crossed the wasteland like a priest and his disciple in tow, walking back in time, to re-enter the town by its aged artery, the railroad.

2.

Eduardo Martinez was conceived during the impatient coupling of his virgin parents, eager to consummate their minutes-old nuptial vows. Here's how it happened.

As the priest concluded the ceremony the new husband raised his bride's veil. Their toes touched, their hands joined, and the moist connection of their eager lips completed the circuit. Holding hands, not breaking the pulse of energy that made their eyes glow with unrestrained passion, they signed in the ruled columns of the centuries-old register. Then, while the priest spread blessed sand to dry over the couple's signatures, the newlyweds drew each other to the nearby anteroom and closed the door. In the darkened room, their desire made them glow like an aurora, giving a flickering light to their lovemaking. A cacophony of sound encased the room and the chapel. The rhythmic pounding of flesh into flesh against the wall kept tempo with the joyous clapping of the guests; the couple's breathless soprano and tenor merged with the angelic chorus of the choir. As the final 'Hallelujah' soared through the roof beams to the heavens, a burst of white lightning shot from the husband's blazing eyes and the soul of Eduardo Martinez swam furiously upstream.

The blush on the love-bride's cheeks soon blossomed in her belly. On the prescribed day a son was born. Eduardo: the latest in an unbroken line of first-born sons of the Martinez family, all with the same unnumbered name.

But it nearly didn't happen that way. Eduardo Martinez's paternal grandmother, Maria, wanted her headstrong first son Eduardo to marry Maria Cassi, the sturdy but not unattractive daughter of the fettler. She had recently met with the fettler and his wife to discuss the terms of their union. She was continuing the tradition of the Martinez family, marrying the first-born Eduardo with Maria, the second-born José with Abril, and so on. But Eduardo Martinez had fallen for the fetching beauty Eliza, the shopkeeper's second daughter. When finally he overheard his mother's scheming, Eduardo Martinez abruptly broke the silent secret of his love.

'What's wrong with Maria?' declared his mother.

'I don't love her,' he said, exasperated. 'I love Eliza. I want to marry her.'

Shocked at her son's sudden confession, Maria stood open-mouthed. 'But, but,' she said, stumbling over the words, 'you don't have to love her. Maria is a good match for you. And she will bring a grand dowry.'

'Mother,' said Eduardo Martinez slowly and clearly, not wanting to be misunderstood, 'I don't want a promised bride; I want a love marriage. I love Eliza. I will marry her.' Eduardo Martinez turned, and with a new conviction, walked up the corridor and out the front door.

Without her husband to back her up, his mother relented. 'Well, can't she at least change her name?' she called after him. But Eduardo Martinez was beyond hearing, already rehearsing his proposal to Eliza.

Eliza: the three syllables made his tongue move in new ways.

3.

Eduardo Martinez, the husband of Eliza, worked as a signalman in the switching and shunting yard of a small town at the junction of several railway lines. In fact, as far back as the records and folklore went, Eduardo Martinez had always worked as a signalman at the railway. 'For centuries! Just like The Phantom,' his father used to joke. 'Immortal. Same name, same job, but a different person behind the mask.'

The life of Eduardo Martinez was almost identical to that of his patrilineal forebears. His father died when Eduardo Martinez was one day shy of his thirteenth birthday. As the first-born son, it was his inalienable right and also his responsibility to inherit his father's terms of employment. So one day after his father Eduardo Martinez's internment, and three days after his fatherless introduction to manhood, Eduardo Martinez began work as a signalman at the railway-switching yard. He would work as a railway signalman like his fathers before him, just as his father's brothers and their father's brothers before them worked and died at sea.

At nineteen he married—Eliza, not Maria—and within a year a son was born: Eduardo. The heir. Now in his early thirties, Eduardo Martinez had worked for more than half his life at the railway. He was two years older than his grandfather had lived, one year younger than his own father, at the median age of the Eduardo Martinez longevity.

4.

From the moment that Eduardo Martinez left the schoolroom he had held a conversation in his head with his father. He already knew the words his father was waiting to say to him. The play for two players, dying father and first-born son, was ingrained in the family DNA. The script called for him to make an honourable response and stand by his father's side in readiness for the handover, but the words caught in his throat, making him dry retch, just like when he tried to swallow the oversized fish oil tablet that his mother said was good for him.

The constable and Eduardo Martinez crossed one line of standard gauge tracks. They continued towards the shunting yard, where a long line of carriages stood, attached to a lightly smoking locomotive. As they rounded the caboose, they came across the last person in a long queue that filed its way along beside numerous freight carriages. Eduardo Martinez stopped in his tracks. The constable continued on.

Who are all these people? thought Eduardo Martinez. He stepped forward, slowly, gazing intently at each person that he passed. The words of his family's melodrama faded, the nameless faces in the queue became unfocused. He found himself just inside the front door of his family home, at the head of the long corridor that connects the front door to the back door, dividing the house neatly in half. The walls of the corridor are lined with portraits. Many times a day he walks along this corridor, in full or in part. And every Sunday since he could walk, his father has led him through the portrait gallery.

'This is history here,' his father began every week, 'your history. It is more important than anything that schoolmaster can teach you.' Every Sunday for almost a dozen years, his father had taught and tested him—in front of every painted face, every photographed profile, the images of first-born sons: the sacred lineage of Eduardo Martinez. Standing at the head of the house, the corridor seemed to stretch endlessly. The first portrait in the sequence of Eduardo Martinez began on the left wall. Eduardo Martinez filed slowly, funereally, past them. He had never met any of them, not even his paternal grandfather—he died years before he was born—and yet he felt as if he knew them all intimately: the names of their wife and children, the age at which they passed on, their quirks and habits, their nicknames. From the first portrait through to the last he could follow the familiar curve of chin, the colour and spacing of eyes, the ever-so-slight hook of nose, the cowlick no brush could flatten, and the dark hair that never aged enough to go grey. Although they all looked so similar, Eduardo Martinez had his favourites, to which he gave his own nicknames. In front of these he now stopped.

The twenty-sixth portrait: '*El Guardavía*', The Flagman. Painted in oils. A proud-faced young man in front of a background of railroad signal flags. Wife Maria. Thirteen children. Age 45 years.

Portrait number fifty-four: '*Encajone Cabeza*', Boxhead. Painted in cubist style by the cousin of a semi-prominent artist of the time (now regarded as an illegitimate fraud). The distinctive family features are prominent. Wife Maria. Eight children, including two sets of twins. Age 37 years.

Number ninety-one: '*El Spectro*'. Hand-held self-portrait taken in low light after drinking too many pisco sours. The print is slightly unfocused, underexposed. He died within days of hanging the photograph and his young son (number ninety-two: '*El Lechero que Sueña*', The Dreaming Milkman) was barely off the teat when he replaced him in the signalman's box. Wife Maria. Two children. Age 19.

The final portrait, number one hundred-eight: '*Pa*'. An overexposed black-and-white photograph of his father, eyes closed, hand on forehead, gripping the smouldering butt of a cigarette between index and forefinger. Wife Eliza. One child.

To the right of Eduardo Martinez's father's portrait, on the right wall nearest the front door: an empty picture frame.

5.

The railway was one of the nation's prized jewels: a valuable necklace that transported much-needed coal, timber, copper and gold from the nether regions of the country to the cities and ports. As signalman, Eduardo Martinez regulated the flow of freight from several remote lines. He imagined himself a valet to the Queen, personally choosing which jewellery she was to wear for each occasion. After consulting the diary of today's appointments, he picked out one of his favourites in the royal colours: emeralds from the Deep South interspersed with rubies from the volcanic plains, all set in gold the colour of corn-fed chicken eggs. He clasped the jewels around her fine neck as he descended the steps of the signal-man's box and strolled into the shunting yard where the weekly XXY Limited Express was soon due to pull in and add some freight carriages to its load of human cargo bound for the capital.

Most of the time, Eduardo Martinez remained in his lofty perch overseeing the goings-on about the rail yard. But one brakeman was ill, another lost a finger a few days ago, so Eduardo Martinez had volunteered to cover them temporarily. Walking into the shunting yard, about to couple the rolling freight stock to the passenger carriages of the XXY Limited Express, he had no idea that he was taking his last steps on earth.

The XXY Limited Express was the oldest in the fleet, the only active relic of the railway's glory days. The carriages were coupled old-style, using the link-and-pin. Simple and effective. An oblong link made from a solid steel spike connected to one carriage was inserted into a tube-like body on the other carriage. Once together, a metal pin was inserted into a hole in the tube that went through the link and out the other side of the tube, holding the link in place.

All of the men at the railway had seen the devastating effects of the link-and-pin coupler: severed fingers, amputated hands, men dragged under carriages that were being driven too fast. For their own safety, the brakemen were issued with a heavy club to hold the link in position. Most of them left it in the brakemen's box, preferring the sport and skill of quick eyes and hands.

So too did Eduardo Martinez. He directed the locomotive and carriages in slowly, slowly. When they were about two metres apart, he raised two arms to the distant driver and stepped into the breach. He had about three seconds. He lifted the heavy steel link near the tip from below with his right hand, grabbed it with his left near the base of the link and slid his right hand back there too. Two seconds. He checked the line of the advancing tube. Good. One second, the crucial time: once the head of the link entered the tube he had to quickly release his hands or lose a finger. One second. His gloved hand slid. The link slipped. He stepped forward to pick it up, stumbled. He raised the link as the final passenger carriage rolled back to couple with the freight stock.

6.

Young Eduardo Martinez was not sure how long he had been staring at his reflected image in the glass of the empty picture frame. He blinked. When his eyes opened, the harsh afternoon light had softened. He closed his eyes, held them closed. The chanted conversation came back to him. He repeated it, again and again, as if by repetition his father's words and his silence could create something different. When finally he opened his eyes, this is what he saw:

Three men standing on the gravel before him, only metres away, the constable on the left, the priest on the right. On either side of them, the carriages of a train. Filing in from the right, a slow-moving queue of people paying their respects to the middle man, his father, whose chest was crushed between the sixth and seventh carriages of the XXY Limited Express.

Eduardo Martinez stepped forward and replaced the constable.

Although he was experiencing great pain, Eduardo Martinez continued to smile and attend to the many people that came to him. He knew he would die. The doctors had already told him there was nothing they could do, then left. As soon as the carriages that held him suspended like a marionette were parted, the toxins from his crushed chest would overrun his body, killing him instantly. He could live only as long as he remained the coupling link.

7.

Throughout the night, the queue of townsfolk seemed to continue for miles. Torches were lit around the trinity. Hawkers walked the line selling hot food and warm drinks. Buskers sat in the breezy alcoves of the joined carriages, their jolly music lending a carnival atmosphere.

Finally, as a thin sliver of sunlight appeared over the ridge, the last in line was received and sent away with a blessing. And so, with only the priest as their audience, Eduardo Martinez grasped his father's hand to play the final act of the family drama. The dying signalman, Eduardo Martinez, played Eduardo Martinez, his son and heir played himself.

'Eduardo, my first-born son, all that was mine is now yours.'

In rehearsed silence Eduardo Martinez kissed his father on both cheeks, released his hand. Without a solitary word, without looking back, he deliberately walked the length of the train and boarded the locomotive. He picked up an idle coal shovel and bent his weight to the new task.

acquiesce

for His Holiness the 17ᵗʰ Gyalwang Karmapa,
Ogyen Trinley Dorje,
and for the benefit of all sentient beings

He was next in line. Finally. He licked his lips and swallowed but the claggy dryness that coated his mouth remained. He put his hands in his pockets, pulled them out and clasped his hands in front of his groin. He shuddered.

The broad shadow of one of the assembly hall's large pillars encased him. He exhaled a cold mist from his mouth and shuddered again. Silent footsteps. A hand beckoned. He pressed forward against the shadow with difficulty into a radiance that temporarily blinded him. He squinted and shuffled forward, towards the source of the brightness.

He stood before a serene young man, a teenager, in maroon and crimson robe, who had recently risked his life and the lives of many others by fleeing the cultural cleansing of his Tibetan homeland to become yet another exile in the Indian Himalaya. He raised his eyes, slowly, as if his chin was being lifted by another, from the young man's shoeless feet to gaze upon the pleasant features of the monk's glowing face and crop of dark hair. He felt compelled to look directly at the young monk's eyes. His pupils dilated. And he plunged into the cavernous cosmos of those eyes: to lose himself, to find himself, and to surrender—finally, irrevocably, unconditionally.

Of course I recognise you—my nemesis, my twin, my guru, my lover. Many times have we broken bread together and slurped wine from the same cup. Many times have I resisted your passionate instructions in matters of the soul, and yearnings of the flesh. And many times have we slain each other at the ford, at the gate, and on the plain.

I can clearly see the bloodied knife in darkness, the fallen King—your father—at my feet, and you by my side, holding my hand. There we are: concubines in the royal court of Samarkan, with green jewels, dark eyes and eager lips. I see myself as a revolutionary tyrant, stricken with consumption, and you my attendant bearing alms. I see plain upon plain littered with the bloody butchered remains of those already destroyed by my pestilential breath, and while the fires still rage through the fields and huts, there you stand like the bronze statue of a patriot in the village common with your hands on hips, awaiting the thrust of my ravenous sword.

And now I recognise you in that maroon robe, reincarnated in your most compassionate form as a high lama, to teach me, to teach only me the ultimate lesson—the one I have resisted and railed against for untold millennia. Your eyes dance with laughter. What do they see? Has the wheel of dharma spun? Have the stubborn karmic stains of countless rebirths been soaped and scrubbed and thrashed over wet rocks so thoroughly that my once white cloth is now white again?

Within a second of their eyes meeting his soul retreated. Then, like a guillotine falling at the appointed hour, he lowered his eyes, bowed his head, and exhaled. At the moment of contemplation, the long, breathless pause between living and dying, the slither of red silk slashed across his neck.

At that precise moment, hundreds of miles away in Bodhgaya, a lone Buddhist monk completed the final prostration of his daily prayers beneath the Mahabodhi Tree, the very same tree at whose base Buddha attained nirvana thousands of years before. As the monk lowered his palm-pressed hands from his heart and opened them like a blooming lotus in his lap, a blessed leaf from the Mahabodhi Tree detached and fluttered and landed in his wrinkled hands. The monk, his eyes still closed, smiled as if a prayer had been answered. With both hands he raised the leaf and touched it lightly to his forehead before placing it in his open prayer book. With gentle firmness he pressed the pages together.

Reflections of Shadows

–shining a light on illusory worlds

There are no hard distinctions between what is real and what is unreal, nor between what is true and what is false. A thing is not necessarily either true or false; it can be both true and false.
Harold Pinter

The mere telling of story removes it from the presence of historical fact; the act of telling creates a new genre of fiction.
Jorge Luis Borges

S top reading now.
  If you have just finished reading the last story, then please, I implore you: do not progress any further. Not yet. Put the book aside. Let the stories settle into you. And in a few days or a week, come back to it, open the book to the page following this one, and continue reading from there.

Welcome back.

In an ideal world, this essay would be unnecessary, and if some felt it was required, it would be located somewhere else. In this ideal world, you would finish reading this book with the final lines of 'acquiesce', mirroring the story-written act of closing a book with the physical act doing likewise.

But in this imperfect world, maybe you might appreciate some explication. But where to put it? It cannot go before the stories—I don't want to prejudice your reading of them. So here it is, grafted onto the rump, like a tail or additional appendage.

Welcome to the reflections of shadows.

1. What it is not

What we think we want is not always what we get, or need; and what we plan to do and what we actually do often do not align. This essay is an example.

The original focus of this essay, as I informed the publisher when she asked, was 'an exploration of the genesis and themes of the stories, as well as providing an allegorical interpretation within the Judeo-Christian and Hindu-Buddhist frameworks'. I wanted to provide an exegesis, an allégoria, in the full sense: literal, typological, tropological and anagogical; as history, linking the story events to events in a sacred text, as a moral, and as prophecy. Where, for each story, every word and sentence, each letter, even the smallest embellishment or idiosyncrasy has a deeper meaning. But can this be done using contemporary fiction as the base text? Using apocryphal texts (such as *The Gospel of Thomas* and *The Apocryphon of James*) as the sacred reference? Is it an eisegesis—reading into the story ideas that have been received from elsewhere, not from God? Are the stories themselves the revealed words of God? Or have I been misled into a voluminous heresy by satanic suggestion?

What it is is what it is. Imperfectly imperfect. As readers we should try not to project our own desires and dislikes upon it.

2. Genesis

The Lord saw the great wickedness of humankind, that every thought and deed was only continual evil. And the Lord was sorry that ... He created humankind in His own image.
    Genesis 6:5—6, 1:27

In the beginning there was ma. And the first night before the first day was dark, full with the blackened seeds of suffering.

But it was not ma who emerged first, but Kelly, and some other unlikely characters.

In 2002, I was living in Eildon, Victoria and working in outdoor education. I defined myself through adventure, and creativity. Bushwalking, rock climbing and paddling took up most of my time, both at work and at play. But how could I indulge creatively?

I took a Short Story unit by distance with the fabulous writers and tutors Mary Manning and Paddy O'Reilly. And from that course emerged the skeletons and other raw material for 'The hangman and the hanged man', 'The uncoupling of Eduardo Martinez', and 'acquiesce'. The stories were shelved incomplete, and it wasn't until 2006, months after relocating to Tennant Creek in the Northern Territory, that I reconnected with my writing. 'Upjohn the Hangman', an earlier version of 'The hangman and the hanged man', was a finalist in the Northern Territory Literary Awards that year.

The major creative catalyst for me was my solo and unsupported foot crossing of the Simpson Desert in July 2008, pulling a cart weighing up to 170 kilograms for 24 days across more than one thousand sand ridges. It charged me with energy and boundless space. In its wake I emerged as a writer. And the terrain I began to explore was influenced by my interest in colonial desert exploration, interaction with Aboriginal people and culture, and the frontier life of the Northern Territory.

But from where did these stories emerge?

For some, there was a specific image or scene, without any framing to give it context. And then of its own accord, without conscious coercion, that image or scene eventually acted as the catalyst for a process of reactions whose results were beyond anything I anticipated or expected. Consider the life cycle of a butterfly. Would anyone who had not witnessed its development really believe that such radical transformation from pupae to caterpillar to butterfly could occur? Was there not some sleight of hand involved? A con? Some magician's trick?

The evolution of 'my abbr.d life' is a good example of fraught process, but I have written about it before. I refer readers to the excellent collection of stories and essays *Cracking the Spine: Ten short Australian stories and how they were written* (Spineless Wonders, 2014). I will instead offer here some other examples.

'The uncoupling of Eduardo Martinez' began as a micro-fiction around the gruesome image of the father's chest being crushed between two railway carriages, knowing that his impending death would not be complete until the carriages were uncoupled. The scene was part of a realistic chest-crush scenario during a Wilderness First Aid course I attended in 2001, with blood and guts and screaming patients. For unknown reasons, the scene stayed with me and emerged at the first opportunity. It suggested the idea of a railway worker, and the railway setting lent a sense of timelessness. With that, and a hint of magical realism, it was not too big a leap to have a lineage of fathers and sons with the same name doing forever the same job, a seemingly endless repetition, yearning to move to the next level of resonance and orbit, and for this to be the moment of effect.

The genesis of 'undersize' was more mundane, but no less immediate. Having returned from walking across the Simpson Desert in July 2008, I was asked, with three days notice, to write and present a short story as a response to a piece of art. The artwork unclaimed by the other writers was a polyptych on paper of a fossil-like mullet by Luke Shelley, a Sydney-based artist-in-residence at Watch this Space gallery in Alice Springs. Write a short story in a couple of days—where to start? Well, what did the artwork look like? What did it conjure in my mind, literally and metaphorically? What would it say if it could talk? And with that last question, the notion of who gets to tell the tale and what would the other side of the story look like arose, and thus conjured was the disgruntled boy narrator. He spoke. I took dictation. But to fit the allotted reading time, I cut the boy off and wrapped it up too quickly with a weak pun. He knew. And so when the opportunity to rewrite came, he whispered in my ear the words I refused to listen to years ago. And so the story evolved into something beyond what it had been.

For the two years that I lived in Tennant Creek (population 3062), a remote outpost on the highway roughly equidistant from Alice Springs, Katherine and Mount Isa, I took notes on the absurd things that were taken for 'normal' in the town. Some of them made it into the town of Koomanjay Creek in 'The Unnameable'; some didn't. The illiterate crows, the boarded up shopfronts, the railway station kilometres out of town where the train arrived near midnight, the plethora of pubs, the newsagent where you could get yesterday's newspaper tomorrow, the sticky bitumen in summer, and more. It was 500 kilometres to the nearest KFC, and people would do that distance and back in a day, taking orders from family and friends, returning with buckets. I enjoyed living in Tennant Creek—it was a great introduction to the easy-going lifestyle and also the politics and problems of living in the Territory. I enjoyed the inter-cultural mix of working with (and for), and playing sport with (and against), Aboriginal people, and learning snippets of their language and culture. 'The Unnameable' was born out of my experience of Tennant Creek, but I could never have written it while I lived there. It required some distance. A few years. And four or five hours drive down the track.

The longer story 'aka' is unlike any other in the collection. It is a fictionalised memoir of actual events. A sub-title for it could be 'based on a true story'. Only the names have been changed. (And some other bits, maybe, but don't ask me which.) This is where I get a bit confused, or confusing. The two epigraphs at the beginning of this essay (by Borges and Pinter—refresh your memory and read them again now) speak to my process and my hazy distinction between fact and fiction, dream and reality, truth and falsity.

What is dream and what reality? What is remembered accurately and what is contrived by the senses or the mind? A dream is no less real for the dreamer—it leaves an impression in the mind as strong as any 'real' event, and sometimes stronger. The Borges quote is an example of how these polarised states work in my mind, because I am not confident that Borges actually said or wrote this, whether I was paraphrasing Borges, or if I, inspired as I was from reading a series of essays by him about his creative process and font of inspiration, made it up myself and attributed it to him because it is something that I think he could have said or written. I am a sloppy researcher sometimes. I have a broad and eclectic reading palate, and I collect abstract ideas and notes like a bowerbird, scribbling almost illegible notes, often without referencing the source or signifying whether it is a direct quote or paraphrase or my own commentary – in short, without the machinations of mathematical proof. The same occurs in my writing, that these 'facts', whether true or invented, mix intimately with an invented world of fiction, and so become, like Borges (may have) said or wrote, 'a new genre of fiction'; a fiction of illusion; a fiction comprised of reflections, and shadows, and reflections of shadows.

All of the newer stories share a similar method of conception. They began as a short note scribbled in pen or pencil on a scrap of paper. That scrap was collected in a pile, and at some time later, months or many months, that pile was transcribed into a document of ideas not yet realised. And there they were left, in the ice of ideas, unable to grow, but importantly, still with the potential for growth. The catalyst for their thawing out was AS Patrić's *The Rattler and other stories* (Spineless Wonders, 2011) and *Las Vegas for Vegans* (Transit Lounge, 2012), in particular, his interweaving of short and long stories with very short stories. I don't know why in Australia we have to make such a distinction based on word count—American stories do not suffer from this same handicap; in fact, length is encouraged, expected. But for me, it was Patrić's one-page or two-page stories that grabbed my attention and had me reaching for the document of unrealised ideas.

'Rats' is one of these. But unlike the other new stories, its genetic code comes from a line in another story in the collection, 'Ulysses of the Pacific' (which is itself a backstory—or sidestory—for a novel manuscript in development). 'Rats' became the answer to the question of an idea: What would happen to the animal occupants of the sinking ship—the rats, the most intelligent of the animals in the Eastern traditions—near the shore of Mt Purgatory? They would survive. They would evolve.

'Last drink' was the last story to be started. I had wanted to write a circular story with no real beginning or end about the cycle of addictive behaviour. Somehow in my reading I was steered to the Italian writer Italo Svevo, a contemporary of James Joyce. According to Svevo's biographical details, he had a life-long addiction to cigarettes. He is the fellow in the story who smokes. The rest was so much fun to write.

But where did I find Svevo? What led me to him? Something I read in the preceding months. I consulted my reading list on my website. Was it Saramago? Or Pessoa? No.

Weeks later, re-reading some Carver, I found out. In his story 'Where is Everyone?', the alcoholic protagonist shares an anecdote from a book that he read years before by Italo Svevo. Carver's story is only in Beginners, the original and unedited text of what became *What We Talk About When We Talk About Love*. For the collection, Carver's editor, Gordon Lish, reduced the story to one-quarter of its length and renamed it 'Mr Coffee and Mr Fixit'. The reference to Svevo was cut.

3. Samsara

The pleasures that come from the world bear in them sorrows to come. In them there is no joy.
Bhagavad Gita 5:22

In the beginning-less beginning—the beginning that never was—there was the Word, and the Word was 'samsara'. And it was as it should be.

But the Lord God would not admit to it being that way. He created Adam and Eve to take the rap for bringing sin into the world. Or blame Satan. But sin and suffering were always present; for what could become manifest from the un-manifest? Sin was there—dormant, with inherent potential, like the potential of fire is within wood. It just needed the conjunction of two or more compounds to react, and sin appeared as if by magic as a by-product. God the creator would have been aware of this possibility, for anything that can occur probably will. His alibi was ready.

The sins of God are readily apparent throughout the Old Testament: jealousy and rage, domineering and boastful pride, envy of other so-called lesser gods, slothful inaction, coveting a chosen people and land, and gluttony and desire for blood worship. If sin was not already present, even in a dormant state, within God's creation, and it was created by another, Satan for instance, then Satan is another god and that which we call God is also merely another god.

One of the main themes of these stories is suffering. And sin (but that is perceived unmarketable, or so I have been told). Let's instead call it desire. And illusion. All are valid.

According to the Old Testament, the root of all sin—and man's disconnection with his own divine nature—is pride. The ego. The rest of the sins follow on like little ducks. But in the Buddhist and Yogic view, the origin of suffering is desire. And according to the *Bhagavad Gita 2:62—63*, 'When connected with sense objects, attraction and desire arise. From this lust arises passion, and confusion, and the ruin of reason.'

I don't intend this to be a discourse on comparative religions, so I will endeavour to be clear and succinct. To know what influences me, and therefore influences the stories, even a little bit, you need to know what moves me. And though I was raised in a middle-class semi-rural setting with non-practising Christian values, I have gravitated towards the spirituality—the philosophies and transformative practices (but not the religious trappings)—of Buddhism and Yoga.

The guidelines for leading a moral life are very similar in the West and the East. But in the East they are developed further. For they apply to not just this current life and an eternal afterlife, they refer to this life being lived and to all past and future lives as well. An ongoing circular existence as opposed to a linear existence. The individual stories and the collection can be viewed in this way too—as containing characters and situations that are confined to each story as separate entities, *and* also as if there is a connective thread of one (or a few) unique 'souls' that runs through the stories of many lifetimes of progress and decline, desire and delusion, from the first words of the first story to the last page of the book. Why can't Shantitia Hames be reborn as Eduardo Martinez? Or Lt Cowper as Raymond Carver's editor? Or Leonardo as a rat? What *samskaras*—the deeply etched psychic impressions of thought and action (also known as *karma*)—would they need to carry on beyond death to the next rebirth for that to occur?

I did not consciously plan to write these stories as a themed collection, but as they all come from the same source, from the same unconsciousness, then they can be read as if they were a continuum. How many variant interpretations of the stories are then possible?

The basic instructions for leading a moral and virtuous life are similarly defined in the Ten Commandments of Moses and in the

Buddhist and Yogic traditions of the East, but they differ in the ultimate goal of human life.

Christians seek to be absolved of sin, to repent their non-virtuous deeds and put their faith in God or Jesus or Mary and in so doing, go to Heaven (via Purgatory) for the afterlife. The sins are familiar to us all: pride, envy, wrath, sloth, greed, gluttony, lust.

A Buddhist avoids the poisonous qualities—pride, envy, ignorance, attachment or desire, aversion—and engages in self-less practices—generosity, honesty, humility, diligence, tolerance, patience, faith and compassion; these qualities and practices are combined with meditation and awareness, in order to have a more advantageous rebirth in the next life, another small step on the path to the ultimate freedom from the cycle of death and rebirth.

In the Yogic tradition according to the *Bhagavad Gita 3:3*, 'Karma Yoga, the path of consecrated action, is the path to perfection.' To live we must make action, *karma*. But to remove *karma* and *samskaras*, one must perform Karma Yoga: to serve others selflessly and generously, acting with conscious awareness and attention. In doing so, happiness is given to others, and in return, the karma yogi receives the blessing of moral purification.

Commonly, what the Buddhist and the Yogi seeks is to truly know themself: to be free of delusion, to be free of desire. The process of transformative wisdom may take untold lifetimes to achieve. To know thyself, know what drives your thoughts and emotions and wants and hates. To know these things, and to quell them, to crush them, to kill them. To kill the ego, the cause of all suffering. This is the message of the sages of India. Patanjali in *Yoga Sutra 4:31* states: 'When the mind is free of clouds that prevent perception [seeing things as they truly are], all is known. There is nothing left to be known.' And this is the message that Jesus most likely adapted from the East[1] into the Hebrew context of One

1. Buddhism was flowering in the Indian subcontinent when Alexander the Great invaded in 330BCE. And at about 250BCE, Ashoka, the great emperor of India and a staunch Buddhist convert, sent missionary ambassadors with the teachings of Buddha to Macedonia, birthplace of Alexander.

God, as evidenced in *Apocryphon of James*: 'The Kingdom of God belongs to those who have put themselves to death.' Not a literal death, but the death of their ego, for where there is no desire or aversion, there is equanimity, peace. And the Kingdom of God is not heaven, but that state of ever-knowing bliss of nirvana, the ultimate freedom.

I see many of the stories in the collection as 'circular' stories. They are like a rooster chasing a pig chasing a snake chasing the rooster in a small circle, each with the tail of the animal they are chasing in its mouth. Greed feeding hatred feeding delusion feeding greed. A mobile feast of endless, insatiable desire.

Roughly the first half of the collection consists of stories where the circle remains closed. These are stories of an opportunity to jump from the merry-go-round missed. And lost opportunities can lose lifetimes of rebirths. For Buddhists believe that it is only possible to transcend and cease the cycle of suffering—of death and rebirth ad infinitum—in the human form. Not as a god or demi-god, not as an animal, and not as a hungry ghost or hell being. Only in human form. And the odds of obtaining a precious human rebirth from a lower realm (animal, ghost or hell) are said to be less than the random chance of a blind turtle in the ocean that comes to the surface only once in one hundred years putting its head through the hole of a wooden cattle-yoke adrift on the ocean waves. So it is paramount that we don't waste our life, that we cultivate positive *samskaras* and practice awareness and meditation in order to remove the bindings that trap us in the cycle of suffering. If we waste the opportunity, then it may be many unfulfilling lifetimes before we get another chance.

Two examples of this are Captain Sturt, the unnamed narrator of 'At Failure Creek', and Mr Browne in 'Encounter at Kalayakapi'. They are afflicted with pride and greed at the very least. Sturt could turn back; Browne could engage with the natives. But their mindset is locked tight. They're spinning out of control and they don't even know it. For though they appear to be in human form, they could be considered to be living in the hell realm, a place where people are skewered screaming and their limbs hacked off only for their body to renew and be slaughtered again and again. And their chance of a higher rebirth is, well, I wouldn't bet the house on it—in fact, I wouldn't put a penny on it.

'Geometry' could be read straight up as a story about a football team that, despite its talent, underachieves. But as a circular story, it could also be seen as a Yogic parable of the disconnection between the intellect, the head, and devotion, the heart, and it requires action, *karma*, by the hands in the form of selfless service, Karma Yoga, to bring the head and heart into balance, and to evolve spiritually. You can do A and B perfectly well, but if they are not integrated, then you may as well not do either, as the result is similar.

By not being specifically named or described, many of the characters become universal. They could be you. Or me. Or your mother or father. Or you in a past life. Or even a future life. And this concept applies also to the timeless setting of many of the stories. They appear contemporary, but that could be the contemporaneous present, the past, or even the near or distant future. Their setting is 'anywhen'.

The time setting of 'The uncoupling of Eduardo Martinez' reflects this quality. It feels like now, but it could have already occurred, or be still yet to occur; they are all valid assumptions. The only clue to it possibly (but only possibly—not surely or probably) being the latter is the length of the lineage. How many decades and centuries would have passed? Young Eduardo Martinez, the 'empty picture frame', is generation 109[2]. You do the maths.

---

2 The number 109 is 108 plus 1, whereby 108 is the sacred number that symbolises the entirety of existence. 108 is OM, the sacred syllable which contains every sound; it is God, emptiness and infinite eternity. 108 is the product of the numbers 1, 2 and 3 raised by the power of themselves (i.e. 1^1 x 2^2 x 3^3 = 1 x 4 x 27 = 108). 108 is the number of earthly temptations to be overcome to achieve the state of nirvana. 108 is the sum total of masculine

A different aspect of influence is found in 'Ulysses of the Pacific'. As mentioned earlier, the story itself is a backstory for the commander of the brig, Lt James Stanley Cowper, who will later become the first European to cross the Australian continent. The story is influenced by and references several classic texts, most notably by Dante and Statius. And it also draws directly upon the hymns and psalms sung by the penitents of Purgatory as they progress up and around the mountain. I listened to these sacred songs repeatedly while writing the story, and I suggest you seek them out (on YouTube) and listen to them as they are mentioned to enhance and transform the reading into a multi-sensory experience. If you only get one song, then get the final one, 'Miserere mei, Domine' sung by the Tallis Scholars[3]—it is sublime. And search out a line by line translation also—the lyric is heart-rending. Start playing the song when it first is heard and the crew's ears are stoppered. This is a very special song. It was performed exclusively in the Sistine Chapel during the Tenebrae service on Holy Wednesday and Good Friday only, so put on some headphones. This song is for you, reader, and the commander alone. For the wreckage of your life, and possibly for your soul's salvation. While reading the rest of the story, try to hit the lines of lyric at the same time as it appears in the story. It is not always possible, but seeking that union was my intent. You may have to read quickly approaching the end, but the final line of the song should be heard as you read the final lines of the story, and as the hairs on the back of your

---

(Shiva) and feminine (Shakti) letters in the Sanskrit alphabet. 108 is the ratio that connects the universal elements of Sun, Earth and Moon: the diameter of the Sun is 108 times that of Earth, and the diameter of Earth is 108 times that of the Moon. There are 108 beads on a mala, indicating the number of repetitions of mantra to be chanted. And there is one additional bead on the mala, the guru bead, which is not counted, but which signifies the start and end point of the cycle.

3. The most exquisite version of the song is performed live at the Basilica de Santa Maria Maggiore, Rome in 1994.

neck stand on end and a whorl of energy swirls at *sahasrara*, the chakra at the rear top of your head.

4. Turning the Wheel of the Dhamma

I have gone round in vain the cycles of many lives ever striving to find the builder of the house of life and death. How great is the sorrow of life that must die! But now I have seen the house-builder: never more shall you build this house. The rafters of sin are broken, the ridge-pole of ignorance is destroyed. The fever of craving is past: for my mortal mind is gone to the joy of the immortal nirvana.

Dhammapada 153-154

This essay has not turned out as I intended, but which part of me had that intent: head or heart? Blame it on the hands: the creative impulse arising from the chaotic disunion of Shiva and Shakti, consciousness and energy.

Maybe I was born into this body a hundred years too late, or maybe my mind resides in the thought-patterns of a century past. I despair that people are no longer educated classically. We lack a common education in languages when we should all be fluent in at least two or three and have a solid grounding in several others, and we lack a common understanding of the cultural landmarks and symbolism of our predecessors. We admire artworks and books from past centuries and yet we only experience them superficially; we don't recognise or comprehend the rich symbolism evident in them. We are more affluent and educated to a higher level than ever before, but where has that got us? Who reads base texts in French or Latin or Greek anymore? How many people have read all three volumes of Dante's *Commedia* (in Italian or in transla-tion)? Or the Old Testament and New Testament in full? It should not be a challenge today to read a story or book that freely mixes language if e-readers are capable of translating text (or if the author's preferred translation is included as hyperlinks). An easy flow of reading should not be given precedence over the needs of the story. It is a form of cultural arrogance to expect everything to be in our own language, English. In doing so, we lose the sound of the song of words in other languages, and we lose the depth of multi-cultural meaning. (But how to pronounce these foreign words? And what do they mean? The storyteller in me smiles and says 'By listening we begin to understand.' By listening to talking books as we read along in conjunction.)

We homogenise creativity by demanding that works of art are easily packaged and consumed. With modern technology we have ever more information at our fingertips and yet we are becoming less intelligent. And many people would rather see a movie than read a classic text.

So for the reader who wants to expand their horizon, I offer a short list of titles, not an exhaustive list, as background reading and references for my mind. Pick one to read and see where it leads you next.

Upanishads
Bhagavad Gita
Dhammapada
Yoga Sutras by Patanjali
Iliad and *Odyssey* by Homer
Thebaid by Statius
Aeneid by Virgil
Divine Comedy: Hell, Purgatory, Paradise by Dante
Holy Bible
Apocryphal gospels of Judas, Mary Magdalene, Philip, Thomas, James

'Sisyphus of the Simpson Desert' is a transitional story. The setting could have been Hell, but it is Hell transformed into Limbo, or Purgatory for the late-repentant. It is a story of repetition, of repetition that is neither negative nor positive. The purpose of the repetition is not known by the person whose task it is to repeat it indefinitely, but that is of no concern. The person does it. They are a servant to it. And in so doing, may become the master of it as well. But that is such a long long long long way off that is almost an eternity.

Repetition is the repeated flow of a sequence of instants. It is observed in four dimensions through memory by running a sequence of instants through the mind's projector, like a movie is a series of still images played rapidly one after the other to give the illusion of them being fluid, continuous. The right mental attitude to repeat a task is to do it as if it were being done for the first time and the last time. There is only now. Now. Now.

After the unresolved stories of suffering of the first half of the collection, and the introductory transition of 'Sisyphus', the second half offers increasing relief and transcendence.

In 'The Unnameable', the mayor is attached to the world of his senses, especially his sense of sight. The blind translator, M, is guided by the more subtle senses of smell and sound and touch. These allow him the ability to perceive and 'see' without his eyes so much more than the mayor ever will. The 'All is Koomanjay' text could be seen as an homogenising desecration of language and culture, or it could very well be a path to the union with the divine, as *Yoga Sutra 4:31* states: 'When the mind is free of clouds that prevent perception, *all is known*.' For M, the path has been shown, or more accurately, heard.

The universal woman in 'The forking path' is headed in another direction, though still unknown. After years of spiritual practice, she finds herself mentally, physically, emotionally and spiritually in a dark place: a place she thought she knew and comprehended. But fire and cancer have displaced her equilibrium so much that she is lost. 'How long is the wandering of lives ending in death for the fool who cannot find the path,' Buddha states in *Dhammapada 60*. She is offered a choice between this and that. She takes this, or that, it matters not. She is moving, in action, consciously; she is removing *karma*. And the lever on her track is switched and she moves into another orbit. She doesn't know what is ahead of her. And reader, we too are no wiser (and nor should we be).

The final story that I will discuss is the final story of the collection: 'acquiesce'. In about 700 words, it is the crystallised essence of *samsara* and transcendence. As such, it is the essence of the book. The story unites two moments of separate space and time to elevate the resonant energy of one soul to a higher level. It is the union of the Shiva consciousness element of the young lama with the Shakti energy of the prostrating monk, which raises the level of consciousness of the narrator.

The three scenes relate to three separate episodes that I experienced, though the story is not about me or my relative spiritual growth (or decline). The first section is informed by a meeting in 2001 with the young Karmapa Lama, a teenager and political refugee recently escaped from Tibet. It was during a public audience near Dharamsala, India. When it was my turn to receive *darshan*, the blessing, I felt drawn into his eyes, and as I bowed forward, he placed a red nylon strip of cloth, signifying my attachment to the Kagyu lineage of transmission and learning, around my neck.

The second occurred during a Siddha Yoga event in Melbourne in the late 1990s. I was a curious attendee, in the gender-segregated audience among thousands of Siddha devotees. During a meditation I saw Shiva, saw him as if he were an old friend. And the large image of the late Baba Muktananda, the previous Siddha guru, over the stage, he too appeared as an old acquaintance from another life, someone who I had refused to bow to many times before, and still I resisted. Later in the afternoon, during the final devotional singing and clapping and stamping, the dormant energy locked away in mooladhara chakra was shaken loose, and my kundalini rose up through the chakras in a sudden shaktipat. I was dizzy, had to sit, my tongue was thick and I couldn't speak. I appeared to others like I may have had a stroke or a diabetic hypo or an overdose. An overdose of Shakti.

The final section relates to the first time I visited Bodhgaya and the Mahabodhi Tree where Siddhartha became the realised Buddha. As part of the moral code of ahimsa, non-violence, the tree cannot be damaged, so leaves are not allowed to be plucked from the tree. Instead, devotees wanting to souvenir some DNA of the tree that instructed Buddha for their own spiritual benefit must content themselves with fallen organic matter. Twigs. Bark. Leaves. The leaves are most prized because of their heart shape and clearly-defined veins. And best of all are freshly fallen leaves. Large green leaves with a full stem and without any blemish. To find one is a blessing. To catch one is a prayer fulfilled. It is a form of freedom from an illusion of the illusion.

5. Death …

Contemporary artists that name their work 'untitled' and then feel the need to provide a paragraph backgrounding the work to give it context miss the point of the title. For books, the title is as far as many a prospective reader will get when faced with a wall of spines in a bookshop or library or the results of a web search. It may be a writer's only opportunity to make a connection or pique someone's curiosity.

As I write this I have no idea what the title of this small collection will eventually be. I have my preference, my favourite, but the editor and publisher may have different opinions. The working titles all illuminate or reflect the same themes, but each in its own unique way. So I'll take you through them, and their reason for being.

For a long time, the working title was *My Life & Other Fictions*. This is not a collection that features the story 'My Life' along with some other pieces, because there is no story with that specific title. Nor should there be. The title infers that life itself is a fiction, a created concept, an illusion. 'My' could also be seen as a shortening of 'Maya'—illusion or delusion (Sanskrit). 'Fictions' (rather than the weaker 'stories') is a nod to Jorge Luis Borges.

I toyed briefly with *Illuminations*, which loosely associates itself with a volume of prose poetry with the same title by Rimbaud, and then for a longer time with *Reflections of Shadows*, an enigmatic title that may be a bit too obscure (even though it fits wonderfully with the illusory and transitory nature of life, fate and suffering).

Finally, I hit upon *The Uncoupling*, a cropping of a story title in the collection, a story that is representative of the transformative potential dormant within us that we rarely acknowledge or utilise.

6. ... and Rebirth

You have now reached the end of this exegesis, and apart from the acknowledgements, the end of the book. But don't close the book yet. I have one last request: Take your bookmark and go back to the beginning of the book. That's right. Go back and start reading again. Because now, after reading this essay, the stories should shimmer with a somewhat altered appearance, like you have put on a pair of glasses where the lenses are a little sharper, and you may experience the nagging feeling that you are reading a book that is oddly familiar and yet is completely new, as if you experienced these stories before, perhaps in a dream.

THE END

Notes

The following notes provide references and background information that may be of assistance to readers.

'Ulysses of the Pacific'
The song of the singing boatload of one hundred souls piloted by an angel is Psalm 114: *In exitu Israel de Aegypto*. The quoted lines of the psalm are numbers 1, 3 and 7 only. A translation of the Latin is:

      1: When Israel went out of Egypt, the house of Jacob
      from a barbarous people
      3: The sea saw and fled…
      7: At the presence of the Lord the earth was moved,
      at the presence of the God of Jacob.

The two competing choirs of sunset sing *Salve Regina* and *Te lucis ante terminum*. A translation of the Latin in the same format as in the text is:

      Hail, Holy Queen [the Virgin Mary],
          To thee before the close of day,
          Creator of the world, we pray,
      Mother of Mercy,
          That, with thy wanted favour, thou
          Would be our guide and keeper now.
      Our life, our sweetness and our hope.

The two songs end with the final line from *Salve Regina*:
      Through the same Christ our Lord.

The declaimed lines by the commander from Dante Alighieri's *Purgatorio* are from canto xxvii. 46—52. A translation of the Italian by Dorothy L Sayers (Penguin Books, 1955) is:

> 46: Then he [Virgil] went on before me, stepping through
>
> the flame, and he asked Statius now to go
>
> behind, who long had walked betwixt us two.
>
> 49: And I, being in, would have been glad to throw
>
> myself for coolness into molten glass,
>
> with such unmeasured heat did that fire glow.
>
> 52: My gentle father talked to cheer me …

The commander switches without interruption to the Roman poet Publius Papinius Statius and his epic *Thebaid* x. 476—479. A translation of the Latin by JH Mozley (Theoi Project – Classical Texts Library, *http://www.theoi.com*, 2000—2017) is:

> … over weapons and prostrate bodies and earth and befouled by heaps of slain, and blood still warm with life, men and horn-footed steeds go rushing: the heavy hoof crushes the limbs, and a rain of gore bathes and clogs the axles.

The song from the mount that causes the sailors to weep and for the commander to order their ears be stoppered with wax, the song that then only he, the commander, hears, is Psalm 51: *Miserere mei, Deus*. The quoted lines of the psalm are numbers 1, 3, 5, 6, 12, 15, 17 and 20. A translation of the Latin is:

> 1: Have mercy on me, O God, according to thy loving-kindness.
>
> 3: Wash me thoroughly from mine iniquity, and cleanse me from my sin.
>
> 5: Against thee only have I sinned, and done this evil in thy sight: that thou might be justified when thou speak, and be clear when thou judge.

6: Behold, I was shapen in iniquity: and in sin did my mother conceive me.

12: Cast me not away from thy presence; and take not thy holy spirit from me.

15: Deliver me from blood-guiltiness, O God, thou God of my salvation: and my tongue shall sing loud of thy righteousness.

17: For thou desirest not sacrifice, else I would give it thee: thou delight not in burnt offerings.

20: Then shall thou be pleased with the sacrifices of righteousness, with burnt offering and whole burnt offering: then shall they offer young bullocks upon thine altar.

The final prayers of a dying sailor are from a lecture on 'Poetry' given by Jorge Luis Borges and recorded on page 92 in the book *Seven Nights* (New Directions Books, 1984/2009).

There are several musical terms used in the text. These are:

> *fortissimo* – very loud
> *calando* – getting slower (*ritardando*) and quieter (*diminuendo*)
> *ritmico* – rhythmical
> *a nessuna cosa* – to nothing; to hold the final note (*fermata*) until it dies away

'The hangman and the hanged man'
The extract is from the 'Particulars of Execution' which is (or at least was when I did my on-site research in 2000) on display at Old Melbourne Gaol.

Acknowledgements

The author thanks:

Spineless Wonders—publisher Bronwyn Mehan, editor Josh
Mei-Ling Dubrau—and all those who midwifed this small book
into being;
Australia Council for the Arts for supporting small independent
book publishers, new voices and alternative fiction;
*Cracking the Spine: Ten short Australian stories and how they were
written*;
the writers and readers of Central Australia and Northern
Territory;
Northern Territory Writers' Centre;
Varuna – the National Writers House, Newcastle Writers'
Festival;
Ptilotus Press, The Red Room Company;
Northern Territory Government and Arts NT;
Melanie Ostell for advice on haemorrhoids and risk-taking,
Sophie Cunningham for *Meanjin*;
Swami Atmamuktananda and Rocklyn Yoga Ashram where the
manuscript was completed as part of my karma yoga practice;
the tarot reader and reading in London, December 1996;
everyone that shared a drink, a meal, a book, an idea, a step
along the way;
my loving and supportive wife, Sharon;
and most of all, thanks to you for reading this book.

Hari Om Tat Sat.

Earlier versions of these stories (some with different titles) appeared elsewhere:

'my abbr.d life'
> *Cracking the spine: Ten short Australian stories and how they were written,* Spineless Wonders, 2014
> Third in Peter Cowan 600 Short Story Prize 2012

'At Failure Creek'
> *Inland Sea,* 2013

'The hangman and the hanged man'
> (as 'Elijah Upjohn, public hangman') *Bruno's Song and other stories from the Northern Territory,* Northern Territory Writers' Centre, 2011
> Shortlisted for *Best Australian Stories 2011*
> Winner of Trudy Graham Biennial Literary Award 2010
> Finalist in NT Literary Awards 2006 (as 'Upjohn the hangman')

'Encounter at Kalayakapi, c. 1871' (as 'Encounter at Kalayakapi, circa 1880') *Meanjin* 68—4, Melbourne University Press, 2009
> Finalist in NT Literary Awards 2009

'The Unnameable'
> *Escape,* Spineless Wonders, 2011
> Finalist in NT Literary Awards 2011

'The uncoupling of Eduardo Martinez'
> *Bruno's Song and other stories from the Northern Territory,* Northern Territory Writers' Centre, 2011
> Finalist in NT Literary Awards 2010

'acquiesce'
> Second in Hawkesbury River Writers Prose Fiction Prize 2010

A Spineless Wonders Publication

shortaustralianstories.com.au

Printed in Australia
AUOC01n0921311017
291038AU00001B/1/P

9 781925 052329